CW01494677

To Maria,

Downtrain

Hope you enjoy your stay in Newfoundland.

Very best wishes,

[signature]

29.3.06

Robert Nisbet was born in Haverfordwest in 1941. He was educated at Milford Haven Grammar School and University College, Swansea. His stories have been published in a wide range of magazines in Europe and the United States. As well as enjoying a successful career in education, he has been a regular contributor to BBC radio and has edited a number of short story anthologies. He is currently a lecturer in creative writing at Trinity College Carmarthen. He is married and lives in Haverfordwest.

By the same author

Dreams and Dealings
Sounds of the Town
Downmarket
The Ladybird Room
Entertaining Sally Ann

Downtrain

Robert Nisbet

PARTHIAN

Parthian
The Old Surgery
Napier Street
Cardigan
SA43 1ED
www.parthianbooks.co.uk

First published in 2004
©Robert Nisbet 2004
All Rights Reserved

ISBN 1-902638-37-9

Typeset in Sabon

Printed and bound by Dinefwr Press, Llandybie

With Support from the Parthian Collective
Edited by Gwen Davies

Parthian is an independent publisher that works with the
support of the Welsh Books Council and the Arts Council of
Wales.

British Library Cataloguing in Publication Data.
A cataloguing record for this book is available from the British
Library.

Cover Design: Lucy Llewellyn

This book is sold subject to the condition that it shall not by
way of trade or otherwise be circulated without the publisher's
prior consent in any form of binding or cover other than that
in which it is published and without a similar condition
including this condition being imposed on the subsequent
purchaser.

To Sally Jones

Acknowledgements

I owe a huge debt of gratitude to Sally Roberts Jones, under whose Alun Books imprint a number of these stories first appeared in book form.

Individual stories have appeared in the following magazines:

Anglo-Welsh Review, Cambrensis, Luceafarul, Momentum, NER/BLQ, New Welsh Review, Planet, Social Care Education, Thought Magazine, Webster Review

With thanks to Gwen Davies, Richard Davies & the Parthian Collective.

Stories

MISS GREY OF MARKET STREET

It was around three o'clock on a Saturday afternoon and Market Street lay grey and wet under the half-hearted shafts of sunlight which only occasionally broke the cloud. A tentative snowfall that morning had turned to slush, and splashed up now and again from passing cars.

The shop fronts were bright enough though, and the delicatessen at the bottom end of the street sparkled just a little with the warming ranges of spirits, liqueurs and chocolates stacked along the window, with the cheese, yogurt, teas and coffees behind. Miss Grey, pecking, tripping, daintily white-haired, made her way towards the shop.

She fluttered into it in a rather delicate way, a slight presence, her sharp, bird-like features softening just occasionally. Now, as habitually, she stepped neatly and precisely over to the stacked rows of Oriental teas, where she pottered long and quietly, in a rapt and quizzical absorption.

It was nearly fifteen years since she'd retired as founder and principal of a small prep school in the town. And more than that, she was Miss Grey, one of the Greys of Market Street, and the Greys had been for many years one of the more prosperous local business families. The grocery had been founded by her father before the First World War. Continued and expanded by Miss

Grey's brother Denzil, it survived into the age of the supermarket as, to quote Denzil's official designation, 'the quality grocery'. Only with Denzil's retirement in the mid-70's did the shop pass to a Swansea firm who, much to Miss Grey's relief, had preserved Denzil's original by-line: 'quality grocery'.

Miss Grey was shopping for tea. To the girl at the counter, this was all part of a rather quaint ritual, conducted regularly once a fortnight. Around three o'clock on a Saturday afternoon the old lady would wander in, her main shopping for the week being done in the morning, and would gaze along the rows of Oriental teas. She'd turn the small wooden boxes, read from their inscriptions, linger for quite a while before eventually selecting one and proceeding with it to the counter. It was all so habitual and so harmless as to create little, if any attention.

But to Miss Grey it was important. She was shopping for tea. She wasn't that well off: the prep school had left her with little by way of profit, and, despite Denzil's devotion to the idea of quality – or perhaps because of it – the business hadn't thrived. Miss Grey had inherited little on Denzil's death a couple of years earlier. But still, cramped though she was by a genteel poverty, she looked for quality, and was satisfied, in the last resort, if she could find it in just one area of her domestic life. Her gaze ranged over the titles on the boxes: Keemun China, Russian Caravan, Earl Grey, Gunpowder Green, Orange Pekoe, Ceylon Breakfast. There was a whole wealth there, of dreams and suggested gentility. After some thought, or some dreaming, she picked down a box of Russian Caravan, and made her way to the counter. She wanted a good blend. Terry would be coming to tea again, and she wanted things nice for him.

Terry, Miss Grey's nephew, arrived about five o'clock, spruce in his Saturday suit, just back from the football match, scrupulously wiping the mud from his shoes in the doorway, before perching on the edge of a stiff and ancient armchair. He looked like her relative. The same bird-like features were exaggerated by soft pecking movements of his head, a slight squint and an occasional nervous twitch. He would jab and squint a curious half-quizzical assent to everything Miss Grey said, but he was still ill at ease in the gentility of her drawing room. It was only six months since he'd started going there, since his return from Margam. And yet: he had come home, he'd wanted to come home, and Miss Grey was part of home. He wanted to get to like it there.

After they'd finished the cakes and sandwiches and were drinking tea, Miss Grey motioned to Terry to stay where he was and went to the kitchen. She came back with the wooden box of Russian Caravan tea which she'd emptied into a tea caddy.

"I thought you'd like to see this, Terry." She passed it over. Terry's large and rather clumsy hands fumbled the box awkwardly as he gazed at it in determined concentration.

"It's the box the tea was packed in," said Miss Grey. "Russian Caravan. Do you see?"

Terry's reply was stammered and clumsy. "It's nice. It's nice tea."

Miss Grey smiled with a pecking eagerness. "There's a story about the tea, on the side of the box. Shall I read it to you?" Terry blushed, but nodded.

Miss Grey was suddenly self-conscious, but caught by a gust of enthusiasm at the same time. She told him the story of the Empress Elizabeth of Russia who in 1735 had set up the first caravan tea trade between Russia and the Far East.

Terry broke into a happy grin. "That's a nice story." He looked in awe at the fragile little box in his large and clumsy hands. "It's a nice box."

Miss Grey flushed a little with excitement. "Would you like it, Terry? Or the label, perhaps? Would you like to collect them?"

Terry nodded eagerly, fired vaguely with the feeling that this was something personal, a family thing. "I wouldn't mind," he said. "I wouldn't mind saving them. Some of the boys saves cards from the Corn Flakes, and things like that. One boy's got some beer mats."

"Terry," Miss Grey was suddenly excited and insistent. "We're a trading family, the Greys. And trade is travel, Terry, very often. Foreign places, strange places. You could collect these labels. There are lots of different ones, with stories of where they're from. Ceylon and India. Russia." She paused. "I get a new box every fortnight. When you come, after the football match, you can have the labels."

Carefully, she peeled the Russian Caravan label from its place and gave it to him. He folded it up, slowly and carefully, and put it neatly into his wallet.

After he'd gone, Miss Grey let her mind run on: Russian Caravan, Gunpowder Green, Formosa Oolong, Earl Grey, Queen Mary, Ceylon Breakfast. A delicate strangeness lay about her mind, the thoughts of the quality grocery between the wars, of the times as a little girl when she'd played in her father's storeroom behind the shop, looking at the labels on the packagings: London, Bristol, Manchester, a strange wide world stretching its beckoning call into the little market town. Phrases and images spun through her mind: of tea merchants in the Strand, established in 1788. Quality grocery: London and Bristol. This was what it meant to Miss Grey to be part of a trading family.

Terry was Denzil's son and had been mentally retarded since an attack of meningitis early in life. His mother had died when he was still in his teens, so that neither Denzil who had the business to run nor Miss Grey, with her prep school, had been able to keep him at home. For over twenty years, he'd been in Margam hospital. It was only recently, with the opening of a residential home for the handicapped in the town, that Terry had come back.

Margam loomed still, in Miss Grey's mind, as something ugly. The residents in the home where Terry was now staying were variously odd, shambling and confused, but the mood was different to Margam. To her, Margam was part of a harsh and howling urban landscape. Patients had been howling, very often, in Terry's ward, when she and Denzil had driven him back after short stays at home. The place was cramped and understaffed – perhaps it was that; perhaps it was the sheer fact of its urban setting. Cities, in Miss Grey's mental romance of trading forays and travellers' tales, meant India and Ceylon, the Empress Elizabeth linking Russia with the far East; at the very least, the London and Bristol her father had traded with. But the urban world of Margam, the first hand contact, was a howling, baying nightmare. There'd been that sad and sour journey across south Wales to take Terry back. And then, quite recently, after Denzil's death a couple of years before, the new home had been opened in Haverfordwest, and Terry had come home.

Terry used to come regularly now, on Saturday afternoons, after his trip to the football match. Regularly, once a fortnight, Miss Grey would peel the label from a small wooden tea box and read him the story before passing on the label for his collection. He must have felt by now the need to reciprocate, for the next Saturday, just before leaving, he passed a small leaflet across to Miss Grey, saying, blushing, "Got you something."

She looked. It was a football programme. Haverfordwest versus Ammanford Town. As she gazed in puzzlement, Terry crowded in his clumsy explanations. "See. It shows you who they was playing." He blushed. "I thought you'd like them. Save them up, like."

Miss Grey could only wonder at the strangeness of the thing. Of course it was nice of the boy, it was kind. So, scrupulously and carefully, she assembled, week by week, her collection of football programmes, read them even, puzzling a little over the names and the jargon. She was touched and pleased by the gesture.

But lurking underneath it was an odd, irrelevant undercurrent of discomfort. In her mind Miss Grey would roll out lists of names of Oriental teas: Gunpowder Green, Darjeeling, Russian Caravan, Earl Grey – lists replete with a magical aura of distant strangeness. But as she collected her football programmes, another list assembled itself: names of opponents and other towns. Carmarthen Town, Llanelli, Ammanford, Briton Ferry, Swansea City, Port Talbot. This list made Miss Grey unhappy. At first she thought it was simply due to how mundane a list it seemed. And then, shuffling a few programmes casually one Saturday, just after Terry had left, she realised the reason for her unease. Carmarthen, Swansea City, Port Talbot. It was the very road to Margam. She realised herself it was a silly objection, no sort of objection at all. She went on saving the football programmes just the same. And all the time she was fighting down her sense of the drabness of the whole affair.

Unease with Terry's visits to the football ground crept upon her in another way. He was getting used to the team and its players by now, and had for a while enthused about a goalkeeper called Cy Morgan, at first perhaps because, as goalkeeper, Cy wore a differently coloured jersey and was easier to identify. Then, one Saturday, he burst out excitedly.

"Auntie. That Cy Morgan. In goal. He's my cousin. I never knew, till today."

Miss Grey puzzled. "Cy Morgan? Oh. Cyril. Good heavens. Does Cyril play football? I hadn't realised. Good heavens, yes. Cyril's father is your mother's brother. I honestly hadn't realised Cyril played football. I'm a little out of touch with that branch of the family."

Terry pressed on eagerly. "I never knew, like. Not till today. That bloke told me. Uncle Randall. Bloke that sells the programmes."

Miss Grey nodded. "That's right. Your Uncle Randall. He did go to the football club quite a bit. He was quite keen on football, I believe. Dear me. I just hadn't realised."

Her unease deepened at this piece of news. There was no rancour, no family feud, simply the feeling there'd always been, among the Greys, that when Denzil had married one of the Morgan girls from Castle Back, he'd rather married beneath him. But Helen Morgan had been loyal and considerate enough, in a rather humdrum and inconspicuous way, and even her brother Randall, known though he was as something of a town loafer, had little that could seriously be levelled against him. Denzil had employed him briefly, as a storeman, and Randall had effectively drifted out of the job rather than actually getting fired. He was a plump, sandy, faded sort of man with sleepy eyes, lounging around town without doing any particular harm. Perhaps Miss Grey just felt that he wasn't ideal as a relative for the Greys, not ideal company for Terry. But there it was. He liked the football matches, and they were probably kind enough to him down there.

Time passed, and Terry seemed to be settling ever more contentedly into the rhythm of his new life at home. The summer brought the football season to an end, but on one occasion Randall Morgan took Terry down to Milford on the bus to see

Glamorgan seconds playing cricket, and Terry brought Miss Grey back a programme from that match. It was signed by a couple of Glamorgan players. As the new season got under way, Miss Grey became aware that the Haverfordwest football team were in a different division or something – Terry said they'd been relegated – and the names on the programme now were of more obscure little townships, off the main road to Margam. Names like Abercynon, Blaenavon and Lewistown were hardly exotic, but had at least the neutral virtue of being unknown.

At Christmas approached, Miss Grey felt she'd like to buy Terry something to do with football for a Christmas present. It would be the right thing to do. By now she'd exhausted the range of Oriental tea labels and she felt there was something a shade selfish in expecting the boy to get involved in her own rather esoteric preoccupation. She couldn't buy him an actual ball: he didn't play himself, as far as she knew; child though he seemed, in many ways, he was a man of over forty, after all. Then she thought of a football scarf, a supporters' scarf. She asked Terry about the colours.

"They're blue, they wear. Blue and white. Only Cy don't, he wears green. He's the goalie." He blushed with pleasure. Miss Grey nodded. Blue and white. She'd have to see. Terry went on talking excitedly about Cy. "He done well today. Stopped a penalty. This bloke shot, like, smacked it, and Cy dived right over. Dived across. Knocked it away, like. They won two-nothing, after that."

Miss Grey had never taken to knitting, although latterly, in her retirement, she'd often wished she had some such attainment as an interest. Somehow though, it had seemed vaguely at odds with her picture of herself: *Headmistress, Miss Grey of Market Street.* So she searched the shops until she did in fact find a blue and white supporters' scarf. She wrapped it carefully and put it away until Christmas time.

On the Saturday afternoon directly before Christmas, Terry was a little late arriving after the football match. When he arrived, a little breathless, he pushed a parcel clumsily wrapped in untied brown paper, into her hands. "I got you something. A present, like. For Christmas." It was a wooden box of Russian Caravan tea. Miss Grey was startled. "Terry. How kind. That really is nice. But it's expensive, dear, very expensive."

She wondered vaguely how he could have afforded it on the limited pocket money he had at the home. It was only when the man from the social services department called the next day that she found out that Terry had stolen it.

The same man called again, a week later, to explain the transfer. Terry would be going back to Margam, for an indefinite period, but she mustn't distress herself. Perhaps three months, maybe six. They'd have to see how things worked out. No, it wasn't a punishment, exactly. And yes, he did realise that Margam was different from the residential home. Well, that was the point in a way. Less freedom. Well, yes, that was the point. The need for supervision. You see, the point with fairly easy access to the community was that they had to feel they could trust a patient. Or resident. But the scheme depended on its not being abused. They'd see how he settled down. He should be able to come back. Three months. Six months. She mustn't distress herself.

The following Saturday, at the football ground, Randall Morgan was casting a pale and amiable gaze about him, when he was aware of a quiet voice, and Miss Grey beside him.

"Good afternoon, Randall. Have you a programme you could sell me?"

"Well, by damn. Miss Grey. Long time, no see. Programme?

Sure." She'd always called him "Randall"; he'd always addressed her as "Miss Grey". It was something quite expected and accepted between them. They were left standing side by side for about half an hour, saying little, shuffling uneasily from time to time. Once Randall spoke, to enquire awkwardly after Terry.

"I'm sure he's settling down," said Miss Grey. "I'll be writing to him tonight."

"Send him my regards," said Randall.

"Surely."

It was the sort of wet, heavy January day which gets dominated, at football grounds, by the dank smell of mud. Miss Grey, perky still, quite strikingly white-haired, looked cold and out of place, incongruously genteel amidst the confused and sporadic noise of about 150 supporters. She turned to Randall after a while: "How is Cyril playing, would you say?"

"Boy's doing well. Dominating the box today. Caught everything this side of the six yard line."

Miss Grey nodded.

"Where can I find out the result of the match, Randall?"

"Be on the Welsh news, half past six. Or you could phone the clubhouse, like. 3511. They'd tell you." He gazed in bewilderment at her.

Miss Grey nodded politely and, shortly afterwards, left for home. She listened to the news at six-thirty, to get the result, then settled down to write a letter to Terry. One of the nurses could read it to him, if some of it was a little difficult.

My dear Terry. I hope you're settling into your new way of life. We all hope, dear, very much, to have you back home soon. I saw your Uncle Randall this afternoon and he sent his regards. The football team played Treharris today and won two-nil. Cyril played a very good game in goal. He was dominating the box, and catching everything this side of the six yard line. I'm sending you a programme for you to look at....

She would be back there, at the football ground, at every match, till Terry came home.

JAM JARS OF SEAWEED AND DREAMS OF LOVE

I met Martha at a time when I was going right out of my way to meet somebody. It was a summer holiday in 1958, when Gus and I had taken the tent down to the Haven with the deliberate intention of having the love affairs of our lifetimes. Anyway, the thing was that we got entangled with a crowd of Swansea boys, including, in particular, one hulking great pansy footballer of bronzed physique, called Dev. We got around to hating Dev's guts so much that long before the fortnight was up I had forgotten any randy impulses I'd taken with me and was talking to Gus of spiritual elopements, wanting to succeed with Martha just to spite Dev.

By "the Haven" anyway, I mean two villages, Little Haven and Broad Haven, on St Bride's Bay, on the Pembrokeshire coast, and you may well not have heard of them. I reckon they're commercialised by now, but it wasn't too bad in 1958: there were a few people coming down from the Swansea and Cardiff areas for holidays, a few fields with caravans and tents, a weekly hop in the church hall, the odd camp-fire and groups of teenagers hanging around the chip-shop and the small café in the evenings.

This was the big attraction, of course. We were just about to go into the Sixth Form, sixteen and shaving, and now that we could go on holiday without our parents, we were all for going where the girls were. We dug out our scruffy old RAF surplus tent, stuck it in Gus's old man's car and cycled down to the Haven.

"You wait, boy," said Gus. "There'll be some really nice girls down there."

I suppose we could have done the job thoroughly and gone to Butlin's – a couple of the boys had – but, when it came to it, we liked the Haven. We'd been cycling down there for years, and when we were kids we used to get down there early on Saturday mornings in the summer term and fish around in the rock-pools for little creatures, anemones, starfish, small crabs, little worms and sea-beasts we never bothered about finding out the names of. We'd collect these creatures, gather them in with seaweed of every kind, and put little clusters of them in jam jars to take home. Sometimes I'd concentrate on seaweeds only: pink and brown and every shade of green. They'd grow, too. Put in a small pebble or two and the moss and the weed will grow on it, and the water will darken and grow rich. Then we'd worry that the creatures would die and would take the jars back to the Haven and empty them back into the pools. We were no biologists, but we did enjoy collecting those sea creatures. So, even when we went down that summer, we took a supply of jars along.

The first evening, though, all our plans were aimed at the romantic adventures of our corny young lives. We cycled over to the café in Broad Haven and, as we parked the bikes, saw three girls going in.

"Nice looking, boy," said Gus. "Look at that one with the pony-tail. She's great."

All our preparatory dreams brewed headily within us: unattainable girls from Swansea or Cardiff, and wild ideas of their sophistication, guiding us skillfully into impossible amours. We were both, I suspect, slightly alarmed at the prospect and half-inclined to settle for somebody steady from Haverfordwest, but we didn't let on to each other.

There were strains of juke-box music wafting out on to the sea-front. The air was tingling with the sea-smells that had our hopeful senses jangling with a mixture of expectancy and panic. The music was pure syrup, dark and lovely, a sort of cry-in-your-Coke country-and-western song, sophistication and rich country pleasures rolled into one. We paused outside the door, nervous now, because the great adventure began here. We went in.

It was a beautiful evening, in a tormented sort of way. We sat at one table, the three girls at another, a courting couple sniggered in the corner, and an old man who seemed to know the owner and have nowhere else to go sat in a cloud of pipe smoke by the door, passing the odd comment about the juke-box.

The girl with the pony-tail really was the country-and-western dream, hair streaming as she galloped on horse-back through my fevered imagination, or spun in a gingham dress through the mazes of a barn dance, like in *Oklahoma*. This was Martha and she really was Miss 1958. She was perfect, and I feared very much that she was beyond me, but went on dreaming just the same.

We did our best to start what our earnest minds pictured as a conversational rush. Gus fixed them with a weak grin and let fall a remark, unbelievable in its triteness, about meeting nice girls like them in a place like that. But they must have been used to this sort of banter in their own town, because they laughed politely and responded in kind. We kept up a fair chat for quite a while on this level of crunching mediocrity, before we switched to the intelligent-discussion tack, considering the pros and cons of each record, for most of which Gus and I were paying, with rippling remarks like,

"Yeah. It's got a great beat," each sharp judgement of this kind being pushed out to sage nods. It was a lovely evening. We didn't take them home or anything, granted, but we had just over a fortnight in hand and we knew our place.

We cycled back to the tent slowly, bemused by this vision of the bright sophisticated world east of Whitland. I think they were from Cefneithin or Llandybïe or somewhere, but that, to us, was "Swansea way" and made them virtually unattainable, giving us all the more reason for giving chase. We had no clearcut strategy – there were three of them to two of us for a start, and we both wanted Martha – but we had all the dreams in the world.

"Better keep those jam jars out of sight," mumbled Gus, as we were nearly asleep. "She'd think we were a right couple of dicks if she saw us fishing for seaweed."

"Yeah, I suppose so." I was sorry about that. I'd planned an extensive operation for the following morning. "What'll we do?"

"In the morning? Play football." That made sense.

We went back to the café every night after that, and we used to see the girls occasionally on the beach while we were hamming up a tremendous exhibition of footballing skills. Our conversations in the café were developing to the pitch where we did actually start to talk sense with them once in a while, and we'd about reached the point where I was considering introducing our jam jars into the conversation, when everything fell through. The holiday season seemed to start with a rush, and, the first weekend we were there, a crowd arrived, including Dev and the Swansea boys.

Let's just say of Dev that he was the big guy and he took over. He was with three mates and they genuinely did come from Swansea. They were footballers in a big way, those four, and somebody said that Dev was on Swansea Town's books as an apprentice professional. I don't know if that was true or not, because he was the sort of character who'd manage to convince everybody of something like that. Either way, he looked the part. He used to flash about the beach with a discarded Swansea Town shirt over his trunks and some flashy Adidas beach shoes, flicking up a much better ball than the one we were kicking around in our sloppy old daps. Then he had this habit, every time he called for the ball, which he did almost all the time, of calling the other boy "son". "Right, son. Through ball." "In the air, son. Float it." "Run it, son, on your own." That "son" habit is a big one with Swansea Town players, so maybe he really was on their books.

He was a big lad, Dev, about a year older than Gus and me, I'd imagine, but brawny. Gus and I were small. Dev was good-looking in a repulsive sort of way, with a semi-crewcut, a Tony Curtis kiss-curl, and short sideboards, which in 1958 were mildly daring. In fact if Martha was Miss 1958, he was Mr 1958, which was a pretty lousy thing to be. And he started to treat Martha as his own personal property from the start.

We were in the café one evening, the night before the weekly hop in the church hall. Quite a crowd was already there, when Dev swanked in on a waft of aftershave. Gus was by the juke-box.

"What are you putting on, son?" he asked. "Let's have 'Manhattan Spiritual'." He leered round the tables. "I like that. I'm very spiritual." He grinned at Martha. "Isn't that right, darling?" She smiled. "Come outside the dance for half-an-hour tomorrow night and we'll have a spiritual get-together."

He really did talk like that. I know Gus and I had talked drivel the previous few evenings, but at least we were bad at it. It's when something is both tripey and well done that it gets unpleasant. And, fair play, we were only corny, when all's said and done.

When Martha and her friends left, they just nodded, to our

immense relief, and said, "See you again" when Dev offered to walk them home. But Dev leered round the café and said, "She'll go, son. You wait." We had the nasty feeling that he might try something on Martha, and we just hoped like hell that she wouldn't want anything to do with him. But he and Martha were out of the dancehall for about ten minutes the next night, even if Dev was looking a big disgruntled when they came back in, and again, didn't walk her home. All we got from the girls we danced with was, "Dev's a case, isn't he? Isn't he handsome?" We were ready to crawl back to the tent and heave.

The second week of our fortnight was a bad one. There were a couple of dozen of us camped in Little Haven and every afternoon it was Dev's game which dominated the beach. "Short ball, son. Roll it. Come on, son. In the air." Big Dev, darting, sprinting, chesting down, etcetera. All the bag of tricks. Fair play, he could play football. Martha and her friends used to sunbathe on the pebbles in a central spot, directly overlooking Dev's game. Gus and I were reduced to rolling short, clumsy passes in a quiet corner. And every night in the café, Dev's laugh, everybody being called "son" or "darling", and Martha smiling all the while.

We used to plan Dev's ultimate downfall in the tent at night, plan to cut off his kiss-curl in his sleep and put it with seaweed in one of our jars, or plan to get the police to impound his Swansea Town shirt as stolen property. And as the week moved towards the final Saturday dance in the church hall, I told Gus that I would just like to walk into the dance holding Martha's hand, walk round the room, dance a couple of times and walk out again. A spiritual elopement. Just to shake Dev. But we'd given up. She'd been playing hard to get, but she'd go with him on the last night. But who cared? The whole big idea of great romances had gone sour on us long before the fortnight was up.

"The hell with it," I said to Gus on the Friday night. "Tomorrow morning I'm getting the jam jars out. And with any luck I'll put Dev in one and pickle him."

It was a lovely morning, that Saturday, and I fried up before Gus had woken. By eight, I was down on the beach with a saddle bag full of jars, had found a little pool away in the corner and was on my own for over an hour, collecting everything, every kind of worm and fish and crab, all the seaweeds, arranging and re-arranging. I had a lovely time. Then I heard a voice.

"Hello, Adrian. What are you doing?"

It was Martha.

"I'm collecting seaweed."

"Can I look?" She looked at my two full jars. "They're lovely. Look at those colours. Look at that little pink piece of seaweed there. It's like a ribbon. What a smashing hobby. Have you been doing it long?"

"Since about eight o'clock."

"No, I meant, how long? You know, how many years?"

"Oh. Yes. For years. Gus and I live very near here, you see. We've been coming down since we were kids. We've always liked collecting them, but we've never known much about them." Then, a bitter thought. "We meant to do quite a bit of collecting this past fortnight, but we never seemed to get round to it."

"What a shame. I'd have loved to have come and watched you. Show me. With that one."

I was away then. "Well, look. I usually start with the odd pebble. I'll take these home, you see, and keep them in the shed. The pebble will get covered with mossy stuff in time. All these things are alive, you see, and breed. Well then, I add a little pool water, not too much, because quite a bit splashes in with the weeds and the animals...."

We had a marvellous morning. Dev and his crowd were playing football in the background, and Gus was watching from the pebbles, half-jealous, but chiefly chuffed at seeing Dev become the victim of my brilliant spiritual elopement. By midday, I had filled all my six jars.

"Can I finish one off?" asked Martha.

"Sure."

"Just with one of these little pink pieces. Isn't it delicate? Look at the way the water fluffs it out."

"It's a great hobby. Will you come to the dance with me tonight?"

There was a slight embarrassed pause, then she smiled. "Yes, I'd like to. I'm going shopping with the girls in Haverfordwest this afternoon. What time shall I meet you?"

"Half past seven? Outside the café?"

She frowned. "Has it got to be the café? I've been fed up these last two weeks with listening to records and people shouting at football."

"I'll meet you just outside, if you like. Then we could go for a walk around the Point."

"Yes. I'll see you at half past seven then. Just outside the café." She helped me carry the jam jars back up to my bike. Dev went on with his game.

I'd been fed up too, with records and football and Dev's talk in the café, but the walk I had with Martha around the Point made me feel better, like one great big breath of fresh air. We talked of simple things, like what we were doing at school, our families, tennis, which we both liked. We exchanged addresses and promised to write.

Then we went to the dance, really lifted up. Martha was a marvellous dancer; she jived like a young foal, her pony-tail flying. We were really happy.

Dev arrived a bit drunk, later on. And everything happened quickly after that. He barged in, grabbed Martha's arm and said, "Okay, son, I'll take over," and I said. "Like hell you will. She's with me." Then there was a scrambly sort of scrap, with the Swansea boys and Gus and some of the boys from school joining in, and the vicar rushing in and out shouting, "Come on now, boys, play the game," and finally picking on me, the smallest, and saying, "You're the troublemaker. Out you go," and shoving me out into the street. I sat outside on the pavement, feeling a bit sick, worrying about Martha. Then she arrived, about the same time as Gus.

"Are you all right, Adrian?" she asked. "That was brave, that really was. He was much bigger than you."

"I'm okay."

"Shall I walk back to your tent with you? I'll make you some tea." She looked at Gus. "Will that be all right?"

"Sure," said Gus, who was past taking in any more. He went back into the hall.

We walked up the hill slowly, and Martha kept squeezing my arm and saying, "That was brave, really." Other than that, we didn't say much – we were holding hands and were both trembling a little. Even after we'd reached the tent and Martha had made some tea, we still didn't say a great deal. We talked a little, again, of schools and tennis. We promised to write to each other.

I was sharply conscious of Martha at moments only – mainly of the scent of femaleness about her. But generally, I was most aware of something rather different: the great hush out in the Haven, and in the bay beyond. We sat holding hands for over an hour, before I finally walked her back to her caravan.

That summer seems a long way away now. The excited and expectant tingle of the sea front outside the café, as Gus and I prepared for the great adventure. Dev, who seems fixed like a caricature, a cardboard man, in a remembered heat. And Martha: she blurs a little now with *Oklahoma*. Oddly, what I remember best are the seaweeds, pink, brown, floating, tingling with salt and sea water; anemones, starfish and sea beasts; and the moss, clinging to the tiny pebbles – darkening and growing rich.

OCKY BOXER

Ocky Boxer, when I first knew him (and I was perhaps nine or ten), was magnificent. I puzzled a little at the time as to why he should have been called "Ocky Boxer", for as far as we knew, he'd never been connected with boxing. But he'd been in football all his life (or so we were assured) and he knew football. In our small town, he *was* football. He was chairman of the local club, a presiding magnate with a rasping tongue and a knowing certainty of judgement. His newsagent's shop at the top end of town was a focal-point for gossip, discussion and conspiracy. Ocky, who rarely did much by way of serving in the shop, would stand by in a sporty check cap, puffing gently at a succession of miniature cigars, while Mrs Ocky did the serving. She was in her forties, frail with hair already turning grey. A cluster of patrons, admirers, hangers-on and acolytes would filter in throughout the week, as Ocky peddled inside information.

Obviously, our real heroes, when we were boys, were bound to be the players themselves, but here we ran into the problem of team policy which Ocky had instigated some years earlier, of boosting the Town's side by importing part-time professionals from the Swansea area. Perhaps three or four of the team, at any given time, would be local boys, town boys, and these we adulated quietly, most of all perhaps Gus Goalie. As far as we knew, Gus was the only goalkeeper the Town had ever had, would ever have, or could ever have. He was dark and dapper, capable of springing on to a shot like a tiger pouncing. Ocky would nod a sage assent if someone in the shop should praise Gus Goalie. "He's an athlete," he'd say. "Athlete, that boy." We'd nod wide-eyed agreement, and later in the week, at the next home game at the Meadow, we'd watch Gus springing to pull a high cross down out of the air, and re-iterate Ocky's wisdom: "He's an athlete," we'd say. "An athlete."

Through the winter months, in the enclosed warmth of Ocky's shop, we glimpsed for the first time a secret, hidden and beautiful man's world, in which athletes like Gus Goalie pounced and wise old men like Ocky Boxer would exhale delicate wisps of cigar smoke as they weighed up situations. Every Wednesday afternoon, Ocky would leave his wife in charge while he went down to the Meadow to chair the team selection meeting. He'd be back in the shop by five, the time at which Gus Goalie, a van driver, would be bringing in the cigarettes deliveries. There would always be a few codgers and a cluster of small boys there to hear a first reading of the team, two full days before it appeared in the *Argus* on Friday. Ocky would start, always, with the same joke.

"In goal," - slight pause – "and this'll surprise you" – another pause and an arch smile – "in goal, Gus Harries." Gus would spread his hands modestly, shrug his shoulders to a wheezy chuckle of polite mirth.

The rest of the team announcement could always produce mild drama, given Ocky's liking for confidential verbal footnotes. He would rap out any surprise announcement with a telling clarity:

"Left half, Cliffie Price." And then one eyebrow would hover a fraction, to precede the voice of wisdom. "You'll see Price on Saturday, boys. He wasn't going to stay on the wing forever. You ask them up Barry way what they thought of Cliffie Price as a left half."

And all the time, in the background, Mrs Ocky was serving deftly, briskly and efficiently, smiling a muted assent to Ocky's wit and wisdom.

By the 1960's, when I was travelling back at weekends and on vacations from my course at Swansea, some of the magic of my earlier view of Ocky Boxer started to slide away. I began to be irritated at the pseudo-cosmopolitanism that would fetch a Town side in every week from Swansea and Barry. Once or twice, I ventured a suggestion to Ocky that some local player might be worth an extended run in the first team. But Ocky's view of me had also changed. I was a college boy, something which to Ocky was pretty well synonymous with "smartarse." I hadn't been out in the business world, I was wet behind the ears. I was prepared to argue with him now, but he didn't like it.

"If you're looking for an inside forward, Mr Williams," I said one weekend, "what about Donny Walters from the seconds? He looks good, and he's a clever player."

Ocky grouched sourly. "Boy's wet. Bloody dreamer. Wants to get stuck in."

Unexpectedly, Mrs Ocky joined the argument, "A few of the boys from the club have been saying that, Ocky. Jim Pritchard was in this morning. He reckoned young Donny was a class player."

"Class player. Dear God. Get you." Ocky had a few muttered grumbles as well about Jim Pritchard who'd been second-fiddling to him for years.

Mrs Ocky flushed a little redly, "Donny'll persevere, Ocky. I like young Donny. He's a nice boy."

Ocky snorted crudely. "Nithe boy. I bet he'th a nithe boy."

I was now beginning to see the other side of Ocky Boxer.

And there began the heated issue of the possible selection of Donny Walters for the first team, hinged on to the perennial question of local players vis-à-vis Swansea imports. Ocky had always favoured the Swansea boys, perhaps because their rather cynical semi-professional edge struck a chord in his hardbitten soul. When a local player was in, he was in – like Gus Goalie, now well into his thirties and still soldiering on – but they had to work to get there.

At this time, though, as the Town tried to plug a problem inside-left position with a succession of rather indifferent players from local sides in the Swansea area, it was pretty clear that it was only Ocky's prejudice that was keeping Donny Walters from his rightful place in the firsts. And out of this came the nasty row I witnessed, rather sadly, on my last night in town, before my departure for Colchester.

There were a few of us chatting over odd times and old times, with Ocky, when Donny Walters came in. He chatted awhile with Mrs Ocky while Ocky grouched in the corner.

And then Mrs Ocky breezed into the conversation, a little jauntily, untypically so. "It's time you gave young Donny a game in the firsts, Ocky. The *Argus* were saying so last week."

Ocky simmered, then bubbled up to an outburst. "*Argus*. Jim Pritchard. Whole bloody lot. They're on at me, till I'm up to here with it. Give the local boys a chance. The seconds. I'll tell you one thing, Mrs Williams. And young Walters there. They played Milford last night. The seconds." He seemed to hover over us all, momentarily but massively, pointing a trembling and accusing finger. "Fair enough. They won. Played well. So I take them for a pint afterwards, in the Farmers. Whole damn team. And what does that runt do?" He was shaking with rage. "Drinks tomato juice. Bloody training, he tells me. Bloody hell, boy. I've been in football thirty years. I don't need a little runt like you to tell me about training." He breathed heavily through his nostrils, before the final snort.

"You won't play first team football in this town, boy."

Stiffly, awkwardly, Donny nodded to Mrs Ocky and shuffled out. And I thought, My God. If that's your local homespun community, I'm glad I'm going.

That mood passed, of course. Through six or seven years in semi-exile, I followed the club's fortunes through the *Argus* I had posted on every week. And what was obvious, within a matter of months, was that Donny Walters was playing first team football. He very rapidly established himself, report by report, as their leading goalscorer.

Other changes seemed to be taking place. A new player-manager (ex-Huddersfield Town, no less) seemed to take charge of the playing side in a fairly comprehensive manner, and the club now directed itself towards a youth policy and a deliberate cultivating of local talent. From what I could gather, Ocky had moved now to the social side of things. There was a photograph in one *Argus* of Ocky presiding at the opening of a long-aspired-for clubhouse, complete with bar and steward. The whole set-up, to my newly cosmopolitan eye, made a fair degree of sense.

Then the ex-Huddersfield man disappeared, for no obvious reason, and the drift back to the Swansea imports began. But Donny Walters was established by now as first team captain. Gus Goalie had just retired (to an apparently beery, photographed celebration, an inscribed tankard, and a long eulogy from Ocky). And by the end of that season, I was on my way home.

I called at the shop. Ocky looked old and tremulous. There was no trace of the old booming tones which had slashed and scarred Donny Walters six or seven years back. He would croak a little uneasily, wheezily even, and much of the time do little more than nod assent to other people's opinions. Mrs Ocky, meanwhile, seemed to look younger. She had always moved about her business crisply and deftly, in the background of Ocky's male emporium. Now it was her shop. Her hair was white but she had a new assurance.

Ocky was also subdued at the Meadow. He had little say in selection or team policy, it seemed, and vaguely gave the impression – as he did in the shop – of hanging around, of being there, welcome enough, accepted, but with nothing of particular value to contribute. A new generation of players had arrived, and each footballing generation has its own jargon and clichés. Ocky was now merely echoing the argot of a generation to which he didn't belong. From the pitch would come the roll of Swansea vowels: "Hell of a ball, Kevin son, hell of a ball." And Ocky would croak hoarsely, like as assenting but unimportant chorus, "Hell of a ball."

Within six months, Ocky was dead. His wife carried on the business, and, on the odd occasion I wandered up to the top of town, I was startled to see how well she looked. She was blooming quite brightly in the glow of autumn, with a lovely gentle red health about her features.

And then we heard that Mrs Ocky had presented a cup to the football club, to be awarded annually, in memory of her husband. We all understood that it was to be presented to the Player of the Year, a type of award which was growing popular in other clubs. On the night of the presentation at the annual dinner, the club's dignitaries packed the clubhouse. Jim Pritchard was chairman now, Gus Goalie was vice-chairman, but we understood that the Ocky Williams Cup would be formally accepted that night, on behalf of the club, by Donny Walters, the first team captain.

The crowd had assembled when Jim Pritchard ushered in Mrs Ocky, received now with a gruff and clumsy respect in what had always been (despite the presence of wives at the annual dinner) very largely a male preserve. She was seated formally alongside Jim Pritchard and, having nodded a gesture of greeting, sat down, looking composed. She talked a little, smiled a little, ate a large turkey salad briskly.

When Mrs Ocky came to speak, she did so briefly and quietly.

"The football club was always a great love of my husband's life. He worked for the club and its interests, but there was always one concern uppermost in his mind. Ocky was on the side of the local players. He saw the need for Swansea players, but he wanted local boys to make the grade as well. So I've asked Mr Pritchard if the club would present the Ocky Williams Cup, at the end of every season, to the best local player of the year."

There was warm and ringing applause, and Gus Goalie, I'm sure, was weeping quietly. Donny rose to accept the cup. He paid a warm and lengthy tribute to Ocky's years of service to the club, and he spoke of his debt, as a local player, to Ocky's help.

"I've been established in the firsts for some years now, ladies and gentlemen, but getting the break wasn't easy. And I owe a great debt to the help and encouragement I had in those early days from Ocky Williams...."

As Donny held forth, Mrs Ocky gazed around her. Just once she gazed across at Donny, still with that lovely glow of health about her, and a trace of something that might have been amusement.

RECONNAISSANCE

It's not in my nature to be driven to drink. Rather than pubs, I took to going to cafes, that summer. And that took me, fairly soon, to Bernadetti's, a little Italian café in South Gate, at the bottom end of town. I went there rather than any other café because, I think, of something mildly exotic in Bernadetti's Italian-American origin. There are plenty of Italian café owners, but Bernadetti is the only one I've known of American beginnings. He had found his way over to town from the States in some rather obscure way just after the war, and had exuded an extravagant presence in his South Gate café ever since. To one like myself, fresh from five years in Swansea art college, with its own small-scale cosmopolis of Chinese restaurants, French novels in translation and impressionist paintings, there was a curious appeal in Bernadetti's mild foreignness.

It was Mrs Bernadetti, Christina, who presided in the café, with three teenage daughters helping out. There was a strange wistful delicacy about all of them. Half-lovely, and at times almost half-sinister. They were remote. There was an ineffable calmness about the café when they presided. The daughters seemed all to be dreaming quietly of plump bambinos, and would hand you your coffee with a musing, faraway air.

Things perked up, though, when old man Bernadetti breezed

in. Some half of the time he'd be out on his rounds, in the van, leaving the café to the family's females. Then he'd return around half-ten, and he'd be back and fore throughout the day. He was about as ebullient and sociable as Christina was distant. He'd settle with any male customer (to a lesser extent with women, with whom he was a shade more formal) and chew the fat. Café talk. You name it, Bernadetti would talk about it: politics, football, prices, tourists, London, Heathrow, petrol, trade unions, you name it.

And yet, was I wrong? Just occasionally I sensed a flustered, badgered look about the tubby figure of old Bernadetti, something of the caged beast even, as he bustled around the café before the inscrutable smile of his wife. Did he really want to cut loose, to get out there with the boys? I wondered this because there were times when I used to see in Bernadetti a possible ally in my personal roaming artist's quest. What I very much wanted to do was to dig into the very bedrock of people's everyday lives and scratch there for those little nuggets of hope and happiness.

And one day when Bernadetti started talking to me about Betjeman Drive, I was listening. Betjeman Drive is the nearest thing to a tough council estate the town has to offer. "The Betjy boys" have been for years a by-word for every kind of hard-boiled, hooligan attitude. And then Bernadetti started singing their praises.

"I tell you, boy. They get at Betjy, they put them down there." He grinned at me. "I'll tell you this. I've been taking that van round this town more years than you've seen; I was going round with a pony and cart before Betjy was built. And I'll tell you this, boy. Betjy is the one part of town, the one part, where nobody'll ask you for tick. They got cash, they pay. No cash, they don't come to you. Nothing wrong with Betjy, boy."

As he held forth, across the counter, Christina was wiping glasses, quiet, faraway, gazing out into a mist of images I could not penetrate. I was left wondering. As another customer appeared, she came forward with every sign of bourgeois gentility, while Bernadetti moved behind her to carry on the drying up. He did so carefully, his chubby little hands almost caressing the glasses. It was that old caged-beast feeling again. What of Christina? She was almost stilled, like an immaculate little doll. Was she a deadener, quietly stifling the old boy's exuberance? I certainly sensed a spiritual kinsman in Bernadetti himself. I felt I'd like to see him out there, on his round, in Betjeman Drive.

Midway through that summer, Bernadetti sprained his wrist, enough to stop him driving for two to three weeks. So he was stuck for a van driver. And I was longing for a chance to work on something like an ice cream round. I offered my services.

"You'll do it? That's great, boy, great. They'll let you? They let schoolteachers do things like that?"

"It'll be easier if you can just pay cash. You know. Forget about the stamp and insurance."

"Do it as a hobble, boy. No problem. That's great. Start tomorrow."

I liked the feel of things the next morning, as I prowled into Bernadetti's stoneslabbed yard behind the shop and started kicking the van engine into life. It was agreed that Bernadetti himself should accompany me, to do the selling, and I wondered about this. He'd seemed very anxious to carry on and I wondered whether he might not have liked to be out of the café for spells, away from womanly influence, out and away.

Certainly, as he emerged from the back of the shop to join me that morning, there was a breezy, up-and-away spirit about him.

And this was most marked, later in the day, after a sort of three o'clock siesta, when we returned to the shop for a quiet potter in the café itself and a cup of tea in the back room. Bernadetti clapped his hands with every sign of relish. "Okay, boy? Out to Betjy."

He was constantly talking as we drove, was Bernadetti, and on this occasion going to great pains to boost the solid homely virtues of the citizens of Betjeman Drive. He was right enough about the tick.

For all that though, for all my predisposition to find the gleaming proletarian worthiness that Bernadetti proclaimed, I was left a shade wistful by that and succeeding trips around Betjeman Drive. They had their money and they bought their ice cream, sure. Perhaps a shade too readily. Too many of the mothers trailed out to us, slippered and sad, buying ice cream and pushing it at little rows of hard-boiled urchins, as if there was some kind of momentary relief in this simple palliative. I was just a shade uneasy about the drab domesticity. I wanted somebody, somewhere, sometime, to get up and sing.

And yet there was still something special about our daily trips out. Come half-past three, every day, Bernadetti would clap his chubby little hands together with a fat, expansive relish: "Okay, boy. Out to Betjy." I'd thought, before taking on the job, that it might be, for Bernadetti, partly a chance to mix with a crowd of tough mates, but it wasn't quite that. We dealt principally with women and children anyway, and Bernadetti's manner towards them was a curious one. He was a cheerful, bluff, insolent kind of small town emperor. On Betjeman Drive, the man who sells the ice cream calls the shots, and I think old Bernadetti liked it that way. Some little urchin would peer in.

"A 99. No, hang on. That's what? Twelve p. Hang on. I've got what?" He'd fumble around with his change.

"Twelve p, boy. You take it or leave it. You got what?"

"Nine."

"Nine. Cornets, six or eight. Wafer, eight."

"Wafer."

"Wafer it is. Next. What's yours, boy?"

And so, in a way, we were setting out on some sort of quest, Bernadetti and I. I found a mutual sympathy in our daily journey, the kicking of the old van's engine into life, 'Okay boy, Out to Betjy', and the vaguely shared sense that we were carrying ice cream and greetings to the people. Patronage, if ever there was, but I didn't dislike the feeling altogether.

At other times we'd reminisce, over his time in business, back to the years just after the war when he'd started out with a horse and cart. In some of these yarns, in fact, I'd find the quiet lyricism of the small town pastoral I'd been looking for all along. Bernadetti and his new bride coming to Wales to a tiny shop, scratching the money together for a horse and cart and bringing a trace of Continental luxury to the simple post-war lives of a battle-scarred generation.

We talked also of women. I'd had a few things on my mind because of a girl friend and Bernadetti had taken this, I think, to mean woman trouble. He'd cautioned me, earnestly and volubly, on the dangers of being too trusting. "One thing you want to watch, boy, it's women. Get the wrong woman, you're down the drain. Don't give a guy a chance." Very often, after that, he'd offer the odd unsolicited warning, when the question of women cropped up.

"Don't you get talked into anything, boy. Get the wrong woman and you're right down there."

I wondered if he was talking about himself.

The final Friday of my stint with Bernadetti. His wrist had about healed. Bernadetti being slow coming out into the back yard, I ventured into the room behind the café to look for him. I heard his voice on the phone, low and cautious. "You'll tell Olwen, then? I'll be up around four-thirty. I've got a lad on the van with me. He's doing the driving. No problems. She'll be ready? That's great."

He put the phone down and looked up a shade furtively as I came in. "We got business later, boy. I'll tell you later on."

He said nothing again until half-past three, when we left for our Betjeman Drive trip, and then he waited cautiously until we were out of earshot of Christina and out into the back yard. "You do me a favour, boy. You drive me to Fishguard by half-past four. We'll belt round Betjy pretty quick this afternoon."

So belt round Betjy we did. Bernadetti was oddly curt, rushed through his business and finished off, as three little boys appeared in the distance, clearly bent on extending our last stop.

"Let's go then, boy. The buggers are late." We hammered off to Fishguard.

He was tense, yet excited, all the way. When we got there, he navigated me through a maze of side streets to a tiny craft shop and then, as I looked on in total bewilderment, beckoned me inside with him. A young female assistant seemed to recognise him. "You called for Olwen?"

"She there?"

"Come on through."

A plump and fussy little woman appeared through a curtained doorway. "I've got it for you," she said. She disappeared, then re-appeared with a small cardboard box. "As you ordered."

"It's a nice one." Bernadetti passed over an envelope, they nodded, and we went back to the van.

As we perched in the van, Bernadetti opened the box and

unwrapped the tissue paper with the same delicacy he used to dry dishes in the café. The paper peeled back to reveal a doll, in what I took to be some sort of national costume.

"Now that's nice," said Bernadetti. "That's nice. Hungarian, boy. Magyar national costume." He gazed tenderly at the doll awhile, then turned to me abruptly. "Okay. We gotta get back. You step on the gas, boy."

We got back just before the café closed, and Bernadetti left his girls in charge, before beckoning me into the back room with Christina and himself.

"Something for you," he said to her. "Little present. Thirty-two now."

Her smile was slow and faraway still, but the quality of gentleness seemed to seep through in a way I hadn't quite noticed before. I remember thinking that at the time: that it may have been there all along, but I hadn't quite noticed. I had the odd sense of sitting in on some strange and timeworn ceremony.

"What nationality?" asked Christina.

"It's Magyar. That's Hungarian. That's good."

"It's lovely."

There was a rather gentle pause. Then: "Shall I show the boy?" asked Bernadetti. Christina nodded. He beckoned me towards another room, a small lounge. Inside there were dozens of dolls, a whole array of them, most in some sort of national costume.

"We came to Wales just after we married. Thirty-two years back. And first anniversary, I thought, get a nice present. We'd just come to Wales. So I got a Welsh doll. A doll in Welsh national costume. That one." He pointed fondly to a faintly shabby little centrepiece. "Okay. Just kind of went from there. I've built it up, year by year. Olwen's been doing them for me for the last ten, but Tina doesn't know about Olwen. I like it all to be a surprise." We went back to the other room, where Christina was rising to go out, lost in a happy dream.

Bernadetti beamed. "Now then," he said. "The boy here. Tina, the boy is having girl friend problems. I tell him, that's no good. You gotta have a good woman behind you. You look at me. I'm battling it out with those buggers on Betjeman Drive all day. I want a good woman to come home to. You believe me, boy. You look what you're doing. You get a good woman, like my Tina." As she passed him, he patted her gently on the buttocks. They smiled.

BARBER SHOP BLUES

Of course it's partly dream and myth. The mingled scents of various lotions, the quietly yellowing glimpses of old boxing photos pinned up on the walls, and I can sense myself back in that strangely innocent boy's world of when I first started going to Viv's barbershop on my own. The flavour of it all, the photographs, the talk of football, and the jumbled array of razor blades and shaving creams made it very much a man's world.

Strands of conversation; threads of dialogue and reminiscence, anecdote, all of which had the comfort of that new world. We listened at home to boxing commentaries from America, and collected cuttings of British champions. We trekked down town to the Bridge Meadow every other Saturday, and we knew, recalled, debated and retold every shade of worldly wisdom from our new footballing world. So Viv's was real. It was close to us, yet pushed out, just that shade beyond. The photos were part of an American series to which only Viv seemed to have access. And the footballing conversations had cynicism and know-how, for Viv was rumoured to have a few contacts on the committee at the Meadow.

Stumpy and I went down once to Viv's shop, tucked away in West Gate, at the top end of town, an hour or so before he closed on Saturday morning. Viv always closed for the afternoon when the Town were playing at home. We were talking about Leslie

Evans, a hard and toothless centre half who'd been playing for the Town for a year or so, hailed originally as a key signing, a recruit from 'up the line', from Swansea. Stumpy's round and crewcut head was poking out from the white cloth which Viv had draped round him and he discoursed earnestly and wisely, retailing snippets he'd picked up from the local Press. "The Boro won't get past Leslie, will they? He'll seal up the middle. Leslie's the iron man."

Viv grinned and slapped his arms down on Stumpy's shoulders.

"By damn, you boys get me. Iron man! Where d'you read that?"

Stumpy frowned defensively. "It said. In the *Argus*."

"Iron man! Let me tell you something." Viv beckoned me into the conversation from the bench where I was waiting my turn, then leaned forward to whisper conspiratorially. "I was talking to one of the boys on the committee. They had an away game at Maerdy three weeks back. Ten minutes gone, and Leslie went down, rolling around, bloody agony. 'My knee's gone,' he kept saying. 'My knee's gone.' Okay. Freddie can't cope with too much in the way of injury, as you know, so they got the Maerdy trainer to old Leslie. He fished out a little white bottle. 'We'll try some of this,' he said. Dabbed it on with a sponge. Give it two minutes and Leslie was frisking around like a lamb. Now then." He lowered his voice just a shade again as I leaned forward from the bench and Stumpy peered intently in the mirror at Viv's reflection. "Do you know what was in that bottle?" said Viv. "Water. That's a fact. Good honest water. And Leslie was up and running like a two-year-old." He grinned, and winked at me in the mirror. "That's your iron man, boy".

At other times, he'd talk across Stumpy and me, would Viv, to other customers, on matters of business and jobs, part of a cluster of potent male concerns towards which Stumpy and I were still feeling our way. Viv was talking once to Archie Rees from the Avenue. "That's true enough of all of us, Archie. Envy the other man's job. You take it. It's surprising the people will say to me, I'd like your job. You're in the warm. Well, fair enough. But they don't realise the half of it. The hours. Ordering. All that. Don't know the half of it." Archie Rees nodded sagely. Stumpy and I sat, wide-eyed, and wondered. We didn't know the half.

But in the warm it was. Life at the barber's shop has the feel of one long winter's evening. The little hot haven of warmth, scented hair oils and gossip. In my memory, in the lotioned fading near to sleep, it always seemed to be snowing outside. We were in the warm, Viv, Stumpy, Archie Rees and I, gossiping and conspiring in a quiet sanctuary of dream and speculation.

Slowly, our world drifted into an age of permissiveness and pin-ups. To some extent, it may have been the way the world was going; Elvis had appeared, along with Teds and sideboards and drainpipe trousers. It may have been part of the shift in our own lives, as we struggled awkwardly into adolescence. But to some slight degree, the change may have been in Viv's shop itself. Certainly, I seem to remember the first pin-ups appearing on the walls there in 1958.

And this isn't, I don't think, just a blurring of memory on my part. I recall a comment by Archie Rees. He gazed sternly at some lavish blonde wedged in beside the mirror, as he settled in the chair. "Where's she from Viv? She's airy." He gazed studiously forward to examine the small print. "Miami Beach Series," he read aloud. Beamed. "All right for Miami beach, Viv. Not round here. She'd catch her bloody death."

Somebody chipped in from the bench on the side. "Keep a cool

head now, Archie. You keep your eyes on the shaving cream."
There was a general wheezy sort of chuckle around the shop, as
Stumpy grinned his delight, I trembled a little with embarrassment,
and Viv grinned complacently. He was deftly chewing on a small
discreet piece of spearmint gum, revelling in the new, mildly
transatlantic image of himself he was now trying to project.

I think Viv's ideas, around that time, were beginning to push
out a little way beyond the West Gate barber's shop. He'd talk
occasionally of getting out, getting out of a rut, taking a pub or a
club somewhere. He'd muse over this, across the shop to waiting
customers, as Stumpy or I sat in the chair. "You take it," he'd say.
"Nice little club somewhere. Out in the country a little way. Have
a bit of entertainment, small group once a week, nothing much."
He rounded from the customer he'd been talking to behind him
and prodded the white-clothed Stumpy in the small of the back.
"Rock'n'roll this boy'd like. Wouldn't you? Not for me. Elvis
Presley. Fats Domino. Not for me. None of your rock'n'roll."

All this talk of pubs and clubs would delight Stumpy, who was
beginning to look on drink as a way of proving his virility. And
Stumpy always had had a vast capacity for appearing worldly-
wise. He liked the pin-ups and he liked the talk of pubs. He'd sit
wide-eyed in the barber's shop, his eyes gleaming, his chubby little
mind eagerly docketing every remark and every impression, before
discoursing sagely on these matters as we trudged cheerfully home.

"Viv would run a good club, boy. I wouldn't mind it, for the
odd evening. Small group, a couple of drinks. I wouldn't mind it."
Or: "Did you see the calendar he's got? By the Brylcreem. Pair of
bumpers there, boy."

I'd wince a little and draw back. It could have been various
things: maturing later (for I started shaving at least two years after
Stumpy did); more of a puritan conscience, maybe. Either way, I

was, on times, a little less comfortable in Viv's in the pin-up age. Curiously though, I think there were times when Viv sensed this mild hesitancy, and sympathised. With Stumpy, he was ready to offer a sly wink as my tubby friend grinned across at some new pin-up. But he often seemed very ready to protect me from such things. I vividly remember one occasion when Archie Rees was chivvying him over some new addition to the Miami Beach Series. I was in the chair while Stumpy and Archie waited their turns.

"That redhead by the shaving cream's a bit much, Viv," said Archie.

Viv grinned. "Good looker."

"Too much for young Stumpy, though. You'll have to strap him in the chair." Stumpy's vast delight was backed by the usual wheezy chuckles, before Archie barged on, a little too crudely.

"And you watch that little beggar in the chair. His specs are steaming up already." Viv's hands tensed slightly, and the atmosphere went suddenly sour, before Viv's voice chopped into it rather thickly. "You leave him alone. He's a good lad." He gave my shoulder a clumsy shake. "You ignore him." He scowled in the mirror at Archie Rees. "I'm not too bothered about pin-ups myself. I only put them up for you buggers."

Viv's talk of pubs and clubs went on, but it never seemed to be headed for much. I remember the afternoon I called in for a last haircut before my departure for college. I was by that time an apprehensive eighteen year old, wondering on the world of the emergent meritocrat, Miami Beach and Swansea, hoping that the town would still be there, unchanged at vacation time. Oddly enough, Viv was reassuring that afternoon, as he scrubbed lotion into the semi-crewcut I'd affected for a year or two. "Off to college on Monday, then? What was that line? That poem? Gather ye rose buds while ye may. You enjoy yourself." He seemed to speculate momentarily on what life might be like up the line, before switching tack suddenly. "You keep to your semi-crew, now. And get a good barber in Swansea." He pondered. "How long's your term? How long will you be away?"

"Ten weeks. I might come down at half-terms, though."

"That's all right, then. Call in here half-term. I'll fix you up. I'll be here."

It was only after I graduated, and took my first job in Colchester, that I was away from town long enough to start getting my hair cut somewhere other than Viv's. I got my hair cut in Colchester at a place called the Barber's Shop, part of a rather poncy outfit known as Chelsea Hair Fashions, with a men's barber's operating within, run by an emasculated character called Rich.

Rich and I were never on a wavelength. He found it depressing, I think, that I should want my five bob's worth out of a haircut, preferring to flick casually with his scissors and comb, to shape, perhaps, rather than to cut. And I remember the almost total linguistic breakdown that occurred between us on my first visit. His scissors dabbed languidly around my head before he finally inspected the back of my neck a little sadly and enquired gloomily, "Graduated, sir, or a line?"

It was a while before I got his drift, but even this incomprehension provoked Rich to no more than a vague dismay. He was referring, anyway, to the hair-line just above the neck. By "graduated" he meant it should curve down according to the natural line of the hair; "a line" meant cut straight across, swept inwards, and shaved underneath. But such phrases I'd never known. The latter style we'd always known, on tougher ground like Viv's, as a DA. It stands officially for District Attorney; folklore paraphrases it as 'duck's arse'. I preferred the way of things back home.

When I'd winced a little before the Miami Beach pin-ups, I hadn't altogether liked the road which Viv and Stumpy were taking. Gazing bemusedly now at the hygienic etiolation of Rich's alternative route, I liked that way a damn sight less. I hankered suddenly for the corny folly of it all, the bragging and the swagger, Archie Rees's nasal witticisms, the grandiose boys' dreams.

The news of Viv, relayed through letters from my mother, was more dramatic. He packed in the West Gate barber's shop and set up a club. He went into business with a rather doubtful character who'd been working with scrap metal and secondhand furniture and they set up a place a few miles out of town called the Skyliner Club.

The tone of my mother's letters was ominous, half-accusing, and referred vaguely, to 'your friend Viv'. There was talk of the odd, rather unsuccessful strip show, rumours of after-hours drinking, and what my mother called 'getting a bad name' – once, apparently, a police raid. I was relieved to get the news that the business had folded and that Viv had a job on a milk round.

I got back to town in time, to a job in the planning department. I was in charge of planning applications within the conservation area, and my new world was one of Georgian architecture, facades and townscapes, petitions and preservation. I'd meet Don Thornton on site with each application, we'd look around old cottages and terraces, correspond and propagand.

Then, after a year or so, the West Gate application came through. Universal Stores wanted to build a new foodliner, had bought up the whole row of cottages along West Gate, Viv's old shop among them, and had an application in to demolish them. Don Thornton and I met on site, fresh from the planning office with our files.

"You could make out a pretty fair case for retention, I think," said Thornton. "I know they're semi-derelict, and being unoccupied doesn't help. And the longer they're left unoccupied, the weaker your case will get. But they're listed, and Universal haven't got listed building consent. You stir it up a little, get it to the Welsh Office, and they could be stymied. They'd be willing to sell to the council, I'd reckon, and the cottages could be done up very nicely. Dwelling houses." He gazed across at the bricks and stone.

"They're significant," he said. "Look at the curve round to the hill. They're a very significant part of the townscape." It all seemed so bloody easy. A fresh lad, Thornton, keen boy, nice lad, but he was an outsider, in the last resort. It was all planning to him, in the end.

The next Saturday I met Viv again, for the first time in years. Stumpy and I had been to the match at the Meadow, against the Boro, and had ambled along to the Carters' Arms afterwards. Stumpy, always one of the world's great naives, was holding forth at a corner table with characteristic earnestness, when Viv came in. Viv's smile was a little slow and weary, but he gathered in his pint and strolled across.

"How are you two boys, then?"

We told him. Both thriving.

"Good. Good."

"How's yourself, then Viv?" asked Stumpy. "Still on the milk round?"

"Left Haven Dairies a year back," said Viv. "I'm working with Telford's, in the office. Sort of admin." He was convincing nobody. Telford's were fruit merchants on a reasonable scale, but they wouldn't have a big enough office to do a lot of admin.

"Prefer it?" asked Stumpy.

"Much better. Much better than the milk round. I'm in the warm. There we are, then. That's the way it goes."

We sipped uneasily awhile, before Stumpy barged the conversation heavily in a new direction. "The Town tanked the Boro this afternoon, Viv. You see it?"

"The Town?"

"Town. Town football team."

Viv nodded very slowly. "The Meadow. I'm with you. You boys still go to the Meadow, then? I haven't been for years now. You know how it is. I was busy, with the club. Got out of the habit, I suppose." He gazed vacantly into his glass. "I could go again, now, too. Lost interest, I suppose."

Universal Stores got permission eventually, to develop on the West Gate site, and to demolish the old barber's shop. I was out there, on the morning the bulldozers moved in.

I've got quite a collection of old photographs of the town at the turn of the century, and one of them shows West Gate around 1909. It was virtually identical then to what it was up to that morning. The only obvious change was the replacing of the old gas lamps by electric lamp standards. I'd been looking over that photograph the night before.

It had been snowing most of the night but was clear now, as I trudged up the street towards West Gate. The noise of the bulldozers rasped very clearly in the winter morning's air. My footsteps scratched quietly along the pavement. There was a curious forsaken feel about the whole damn morning, donkey-jacketed trudging through the snow. I met Viv at the corner of West Gate.

"Old place is coming down, then, Viv. Sad to see it go."

He replied very slowly. "What's the poem? Old order changes.

Giving way to new. That's the way it goes."

"They could have kept those cottages," I said. "They were in good shape structurally." Planners' talk.

"Best bloody thing that could happen," said Viv. "Best bloody thing." His tone became suddenly urgent. "I'll tell you something. Somebody showed me a photograph a couple of days back. This street in 1909 or something. Seventy years ago. And you take out the gas lamps, put the electric in and nothing had changed. Nothing had changed in seventy bloody years. Progress, this town needs. Progress."

The heavy grumble of the bulldozers was sharp. I was aware of the sad, damp flecks of tears running quietly down Viv's face, before he marched off abruptly down the snow-stained street.

TIME TO GO HOME

I had taken a dislike to Cardiff as that winter wore on, and liked it even less that grey and gloomy December evening. Rain drizzled into the corners of seedy little streets, flapped against wet and aimlessly garish hoardings, and misery drizzled over all, the city's misery and my own. I decided to go home for the weekend.

I had parked outside the station and walked down there from the bus stop, hunching my shoulders against the slowly soaking greyness. There was a rail strike on that evening and I watched the odd desultory passenger standing around outside the station, waiting for a chance to get away.

Angela was sheltering forlornly just inside the station entrance. The sight of her caught me with a sense of loss that shook abruptly in my stomach. But the feeling was real and bright in a way, more than the grey wistfulness of what I felt in Cardiff.

I realised that she must be feeling nervous; she had always been prone to brief but unpleasant attacks of nervous exhaustion. We hadn't communicated at all in the year and more since our engagement broke up, but those attacks were sharp. She looked lost and lonely, leaning against a time-table, one hand clutching the side, tensing itself occasionally.

As I approached, she gazed at me, showing little reaction as I took her elbow.

"Aren't you feeling well?"

She smiled rather sadly. "Hello, Tim."

"One of your attacks?"

"It'll be all right in a moment. Thank you."

"Come and have some tea."

"Thank you."

We moved off in a vague dream, through the murk of the early evening. I led her carefully to the buffet, ordered some tea and sat her in a corner. She leaned back and closed her eyes. She had always had this tendency, in times of stress, to react with such brief attacks. She would have been visiting Miranda. She drank some tea and, slowly calmed down.

"Feeling better?"

"Yes, thanks. It was very kind of you to help."

She waited for me to respond and I tried to shrug it off.

"Don't be silly. You can't leave friends... I hope we're still friends."

She looked down and fiddled with her spoon. "Yes, of course. I hope so."

"Would you like another cup?"

"Please."

"You don't mind if I have a bottle of beer to keep you company?" Which was a silly thing to ask; how could she mind?

"No, of course not."

I tried to be brazen. She looked so sad. "I still think that a glass of brandy would be best for your attacks."

She did smile slightly. "I know you do. And probably you're right. But you know I'll have tea, don't you?"

I nodded, ordered a tea and a bottle of brown as the waitress came round. "I'll enjoy a second cup of tea," she said. Then we were silent again. I fidgeted with the cutlery in front of me; she stirred aimlessly in the bottom of her first tea-cup. Then I remembered the rail strike.

"How are you getting home, Angela?" I asked.

"There'll be a train about eight. As far as Carmarthen, anyway. My father would fetch me from there."

"I've got my car outside. I can give you a lift."

She looked up, a little bewildered. "I'm going home for the weekend," I said. "Please come with me. You'll have nearly three hours to wait, and this is a miserable place." She was still hesitant. "I'd be very glad if you'd come. I'd hate to think of you waiting here. It seems ridiculous."

She still looked worried, but relieved also. "If you're sure you don't mind."

"Of course I don't mind."

Then she smiled and seemed to relax. "Thank you, Tim. It would make things a lot simpler."

Then the tea and beer arrived and we lapsed again into silence. I thought I would have to ask about Miranda but I was half-afraid I might upset her again. I risked it. I was concerned for her and wanted to show it.

"Have you been visiting Miranda?"

She nodded.

"How was she?"

"Much as usual. She'll never improve much, I realize that now. But she always recognises me and I think she does enjoy my visits." She smiled tightly. Had we been still courting, she would have cried and this would have been some relief to her. She drank the tea and then, with a visible effort, changed the subject. I was glad I'd asked; it was over now.

"What are you doing in Cardiff, Tim? Do you live here now?"

"Yes. I work here. Lecturing."

"Really? In the university?"

"No. A polytechnic."

"Oh, good. Do you like it?"

"I don't know. I don't think so. But perhaps it's just my mood this evening. It's grey and miserable. So I thought I'd go home for the weekend."

"Did you get your MA afterwards?"

"Yes, that was all right."

"Good."

Then we got the bill, I paid and we left. I walked beside Angela in the gloom, feeling the odd impulse to put an arm around her waist, nuzzle her gently, comfort. It was the same car as I'd had as a student, a shabby, second-hand Morris 1000, and I wondered if the cluster of memories clinging around its faded leather would worry her. It seemed to have the opposite effect. I sensed the flickering of the impish gaiety that, when we were courting, seemed to bubble up out of Angela's intensity. She settled in the passenger seat beside me and smiled. "It's a nice car," she said.

Then the windscreen wipers flicked some of the rain away and we moved slowly out of Cardiff as the very grey, wet night closed in. We drove out in silence down the Cowbridge Road.

"Are you really unhappy in your job, Tim?" she asked. "I'd have thought it would have suited you."

"In what way?" I asked, interested. "In that I can talk all day and get paid for it?"

"Without being nasty, yes. You can talk about books, anyway. You like that."

"Yes, I suppose it's a good enough job. But..." There was that feeling then, how much should I confide? I had once confided impossible dreams in Angela. "I think part of the trouble is that I don't like Cardiff. I don't like cities. They're big and harsh."

"Why not get a job somewhere else?"

"Well, polytechnics are all in cities, pretty well. You know the saying – you've got to go where the jobs are."

"Have you?" This was the impish side of Angela, sure enough.

I couldn't resist the next sharp comment: "I suppose when I went to Cardiff, I was being practical."

She flushed and said nothing.

"I'm sorry," I said. "I didn't mean to be nasty. I was getting at myself, anyway." And I did feel like getting at myself. Angela reminded me of all I had once hoped for. She had been a part of it all and a part of a life that was brighter than this grey city life of the academic hack. The rain drummed quietly on the roof of the car as we followed the headlights further west, on towards Bridgend. The wipers flopped quietly and steadily on the screen before us. Still it drizzled and the dark was thick by now. Okay. So I would confide. There was a pause, and I felt like someone preparing to make a speech.

"I remember saying to you once – a while ago – that after I finished my MA, I'd come back to Haverfordwest and have a dual career: a poet and a shoe-shine boy. Or a bread roundsman or van driver, or something."

"I remember." She showed no reaction.

"Well... I wish I had, in a way. You know, the things I used to say. Prophet of the common man. I was a bit wild and daft, I suppose, but I wish it had worked out. That's what I meant about being practical. In real life, you don't do things like that. You go to a polytechnic in Cardiff and earn a regular salary."

"I know," she said. "It's a pity."

The car surged on; not far to Port Talbot. Slowly our ghosts drag home. Now why had that line from Wilfred Owen come into my mind? There was nothing slow about the way this conversation was building up. We were being startlingly familiar, for a separated couple; my hands were trembling slightly on the steering-wheel. It was the car – the same car in which we'd sat so often as a courting couple. But the journey did have that feel about it, a return journey of two lost spirits: a long, gloomy road, winding away into the dark, a flickering haven of warmth and light behind the grey wet windscreen, and Angela and I huddling into it for warmth and comfort. We were quiet for a while.

"Did you enjoy the MA in the end?" Angela asked suddenly. "It worked out all right?"

"Yes, I think so. It was a little fanciful and strained, perhaps."

"In what way?"

"Well, this does happen in academic work. You set out to establish your idea and see it everywhere. But... well, do you remember? I explained once the idea I was working on."

"Yes. The young romantic poet getting tough and then – what? – getting back to his early ideas in a tougher sort of way."

She obviously remembered very clearly. And suddenly we were talking, very much as we used to, about Wilfred Owen, my explaining what intrigued me: the young aesthete, flirting with soft Keatsian melodies in the summer of 1914; all hell breaking loose around him; crude verse, harsh and ugly, forced on him as the only sensible possibility; then a slow struggle to impose a genuine romantic vision on his experience. I told Angela of what I felt I had established in the end: the Hyperion echoes in "Strange Meeting" and all the rest of it. Finally, the fanciful bit: the profound dull tunnel of "Strange Meeting" as a necessary abyss into which Owen was pushed and from which he emerged with a newer, purer vision of himself and a deeper, truer romanticism. The car plunged onwards through the night.

"Is that true of all poets?" asked Angela. "And dreamers? Do they all have to be toughened?"

I tried to focus on the question and to pick out the road in the wet dark stretching in front of the headlights. "I think that's the sort of thing I should be asking," I said, thinking aloud, "particularly as I regard myself as a poet. But the stupid thing with academic life is that you sometimes get too close to a particular problem and don't relate it to yourself. I don't know. I really hadn't thought."

"What would you make of this rain? If you were going to write a poem about it."

"Why this rain? What's that got to do with toughening?"

"Well, you said you didn't like Cardiff and it doesn't sound as if you like your job altogether. So would you describe the rain as weeping?"

I couldn't be sure if she was curious or sarcastic. Most of the poems I'd written when I knew her had involved weeping at some stage. I grinned off my embarrassment. "That would be a little obvious, wouldn't it?"

There was a pause, during which Angela seemed to be a little nervous, preparing, I felt, to say something risky. She spoke, huskily. "What was that line from Wilfred Owen you particularly liked?"

"Probably the one from "Insensibility": the eternal reciprocity of tears."

"And what did you say it meant?"

I was aware of being got at. "Well... the way people are linked by their sorrows. Share them."

She smiled. "You wrote a lot about weeping then, didn't you?"

"Yes." I was embarrassed.

"And I thought sometimes it was rather silly. But I was the one who wept." About Miranda, she might have added. About the other things we didn't share. About our arguments.

A little later, her voice shaking slightly, she asked "What sort of poem would you make up about those lights?"

Port Talbot steelworks were to our left, a lurid and Satanic glow, looming fiercely in the misty darkness. "About warmth," I said quickly. "Somebody else's. Being passed by. Other people live there and it's home to them, light and heat. We've got a long way to go."

We were both tense now and drove with relief into the dark, away from the unreal glare of the steelworks. The conversation unwound and we talked more casually for some while, of odd people around town, who'd married who; things of that kind.

Then we were driving through Penllergaer and I nodded to a turning to our left. "Down to Sketty Lane that way," I said.

"Does it bring back memories?" she asked.

"Yes. I enjoyed my time at Swansea, particularly the early days. I liked being a bookish dreamer."

"What are you now, then?"

"A bookish businessman." That was the first time I'd thought of that phrase.

"What do you mean?" she asked.

"Well, books are getting to be a business for me. I've finished the MA, now I'm thinking of a research paper, because it's expected, and I wish sometimes I could take books a little more casually. Lazily, even. And step back and look at them and the world."

"How do you mean?"

"Well, I don't think I ever apply what I find out. Take tonight. I spent two years deciding that Wilfred Owen's romanticism improved by being toughened by experience. Then you asked me if any poet's did – or mine did – and I hadn't thought."

"Do you still write poetry?" she asked.

"Yes," I said. "Thank God."

"Well, have your ideals changed?"

"I sometimes wonder if I ever had any."

"Yes, you did." Her voice was very soft. "You were very idealistic when I first met you."

We paused briefly, then I said, "Remind me."

"You just wanted to live for dreams and poems. I was always telling you to be more practical." Her voice was barely audible now. "I hope I didn't kill anything in you."

Hearing this sad, appealing tone, I wanted desperately to reassure her, to let her know that my own sour folly shouldn't be visited on her.

"Don't be silly, Angela," I said. "A lot of my ideas then were just adolescent fancies. It was a long, hot summer and any damn fool can lounge on the beach and talk like that."

"But you were serious about some things."

"Such as?"

Her voice was very quiet. "Homes," she said. "Nice homes."

Yes. My hands were trembling on the steering-wheel again. What was she trying to get at? That I'd matured and wanted nothing better now than a nice home and garden, etcetera, etcetera?

"I still feel the same, I think," I said slowly, "Homes are for people, not people for homes. You should do your house up as it suits you. If people enjoy hours of gardening, they should garden. If they prefer writing poems, they should write poems instead."

"Yes," she said suddenly. "I came to feel all that after... later on. Well, not just that. The other things you'd said. About the word 'nice'." She looked across at me, as if for help.

"Yes," I said, "but every student has it in for the word 'nice'. Down with bourgeois morality and so forth."

"No," she said, again abruptly. "You were right. Do you remember... you once said, poets see more clearly sometimes. Other people may act more on what they believe, but poets sometimes aren't so busy acting and have more time to get things in perspective." The words were tumbling from her. "Well, I still like plenty of things that one would call 'nice', but I don't just want everything 'nice' as some sort of ideal in itself. Miranda isn't 'nice', I suppose, but if people think I should forget about her, I won't. So to hell with the rest of the world, just as you said. I'll go my own way, a poet's way even... only...." And she stopped, trembling.

Only, yes. I felt the force of the ironic reproach she hadn't intended. The poet's way, only I, the poet, had been reluctant to get involved with Miranda, because it was too much effort. Just at this point Angela, not I, would plunge into what I had once flamboyantly described as the sewer of life. She would weep.

We were getting tense again. The roads in that part of East Carmarthenshire were difficult to pick out sometimes and I tried hard to concentrate on the road. We talked more quietly of my job. I mentioned a colleague who genuinely was a poet, of some note, a man who had helped me a great deal. I mentioned evenings spent at his home, talking of poems and ideas.

"What is his home like?" Angela asked.

"I'd never thought of that. Nice enough, I suppose. 'Pleasant' would be a better word. You know, they wash up and polish the place and so on. I don't think he slogs at it, or anything, though."

I wondered about this, as we drove on in silence behind the quiet, steady flapping of the windscreen wipers. "But the thing is that I hadn't thought of it. It's not really vital either way. I go there to meet them."

"Yes," she said. "I didn't mean to pry. I just wondered if a poet's home was so much different from anybody else's."

"No, it isn't really."

"Are poets different? From other people?"

"It depends what you mean by 'poets'. I think the word should cover people who are sensitive." I felt uncomfortable, guilty even. "I think you can have a sort of poetic, or intuitive grasp of life. That's probably what I meant by being a poet. Being idealistic, I suppose. Looking further than the obvious, and possessions and all the rest."

She smiled. "So you haven't changed so very much?"

"Not in that way, no."

Then she stopped smiling and looked at me, worried, "But … what about all that earlier? Your job in Cardiff? Being practical and going where the jobs are?"

Again, she was forcing me to look uncomfortably close at myself. Did she mean, should I just opt out? Be a poet and a shoe-shine boy. She was watching me think, wondering. "I *would* like to come back to Pembrokeshire, and it probably is the feeling that it would be impractical that stops me. I don't know – it's easier to talk of being a shoe-shine boy when you're a student."

"But you know it's not that drastic, Tim, surely. There are jobs in Haverfordwest. Practical possibilities." She grinned brightly. "You'd have got tired of shoe-shining after a while."

"I might come back, I think," I said, "yes."

We drove on in silence, past the wharf at Carmarthen and on up through the town, past a few house-lights which sparkled in the darkness.

"It's been a miserable winter," she said.

"Yes." I said. "I think that's partly why I decided to come home this weekend." I pondered about this. "I think going home in the winter appeals to me more, but it makers me more wistful, in a way."

"Why?"

"Well, for years I've been in Haverfordwest mainly in the summer. Then it's easy, everything is in high-holiday mood, and you can lie out on the beaches, talking about anything. But when it's time to go away again in the autumn, I feel that the real life is going to go on and I'll be leaving it behind. Then, when I visit it in the winter, I think of what I might have missed while I was away."

"What sort of things?"

"The everyday life. It's the old idea I always had, I suppose: the poet as a small-town prophet."

"How exactly would you be that? In practice?"

"I suppose, mainly, by living to the full. It's my Owen MA idea in a way, I suppose. The early idealism, all romance and sunshine, only being worth anything when it toughens. You've got to live first."

"Yes." She just sat quietly. Driving in that rain had been strenuous, and there was a roadside restaurant coming up in St. Clears.

"Let's have a cup of tea and something to eat," I said.

The restaurant was warm and cheerful. For the first time that evening, we were sitting comfortably, in warm light, a cocoon of mild ease wrapping us away from the wind and the rain outside.

"What sort of home would you like, Angela?" I asked.

"A pleasant one. One for the people in it."

"And a tough one? Tough enough to take the eternal reciprocity of tears?"

"Yes, it would have to be tough enough for people to weep there when they had to."

"Yes."

We smiled. "Have you proposed again now?" she asked.

"Yes."

"And I've accepted."

We ate scones in silence, resting in the warmth. It had been a tiring journey and we still had twenty miles to go. Then, when we were nearly finished, I mentioned an idea that seemed to make sense of a lot of what we'd said.

"I think that the words 'home' and 'love' have a lot in common," I said. "In some ways, they're almost the same word. A home should be a loving place, before anything else. In a way…

She raised a hand to stop me. "No need to say any more." We finished the tea quietly.

It was getting late now. "Come on," I said, "it's time to go home."

THE LADYBIRD ROOM

"If I may lapse into the vernacular," said Webster, "I should call them snotty-nosed little gits." This brief attempt at whimsy seemed to be too much for him to sustain, for he then burst onwards aggressively. "It's the old grammar school ethic. They are the elite. And we can't let it go unchecked. We want a caring community."

He ground his way out of the staff room aggrievedly, his sallow cheeks flushed, his greasy hair flashing. He talked like that very often, his caring clichés interspersed with a crudity that was perhaps designed to appeal to his earthier colleagues, to show that Webster too was one of the boys.

Which in fact he wasn't. When we'd established our new comprehensive school a couple of months earlier, most of us had variously drifted, bumbled and wheezed our way into the new establishment from the previous grammar and modern schools. Webster though was an import, a new appointment from outside, designed, we suspected, as a salutary reminder to us all that there was a new and intense professionalism abroad, a sharp and rasping edge to the comprehensive experience. For Webster was the deputy head in charge of matters pastoral, and it seemed that his mandate from on high was to create in our midst a caring community.

The snag was that the community didn't greatly care for

Webster. The sceptics among us were inclined to regard him as some kind of con-man who'd nailed his colours to the caring mast for want of any other which might be readily available. Killer, who'd spent nearly thirty years teaching maths in the old grammar school and was, if we're honest, a shade too old for escapades like a new comprehensive school, was prone to mutter, only *semi-sotto voce*, when someone came to the staff room door for Webster, "He can't see you today, laddie. Mr Webster is too busy with his thesis on pastoral care to look after you buggers."

Unfortunately, I wasn't quite in Killer's position. I was some sort of Sixth Form assistant tutor in the new school, and had a future to make. Which was why Webster's recent salvo, aimed as it was at the Sixth Form, had caught me a little on the hop. It had been his plan to harangue the Sixth Form and drum up volunteers for a support reading scheme. The idea was that Sixth Formers should go along individually in odd free periods and listen to slower readers in the First Form, offering a little encouragement and a sympathetic ear.

Now, to be honest, I was all for it. It was disappointing that Webster's appeal had produced a nil return. And it was particularly disappointing because already our Sixth Form (ex-grammar school kids for the most part) were under fire in many quarters for being elitist snobs. It was a pity. I liked them by and large, and suspected that they probably weren't snobbish at all. I felt they were, like many of their elders, a little daunted by the academic upheaval that had bounced so recently about their ears, and inclined to retreat from it suspiciously. I also felt they were dubious about Webster in particular – weren't we all?

I decided to add a personal appeal to Webster's unsuccessful venture and, the following morning, spoke to our Sixth Form Assembly and asked for volunteers. This seemed to have worked, partly because I fancy my style of address, being essentially bumbling and disorganised, strikes more of a chord in a communal Sixth Form bosom than would Webster's shafts of rhetoric. The first person to respond, some half-an-hour after the assembly, was Sarah Meacham, who had a lovely smile and a liking for netball. She volunteered the information that she'd been a Sunday-school teacher, wanted to train as an infant teacher, and what did I reckon – would she be any good?

"Of course you would, Sarah. We're told now there's no special technique involved with very slow readers. It's just patience and a sympathetic ear. And it's one to one, so you wouldn't have any disciplinary tangles – or if you did, you could let us know straight away. Fine. Shall I give your name to Mr Webster, then?"

"Yes, please. And you could ask Abigail and Helen. They might be keen."

"Fine, thanks."

By the end of the morning, I had twelve names and took my list to Webster, who contrived to eye both me and the list suspiciously. "Right, I see. Oh well, there we are. Twelve, you say? Yes, that'll be all right. I'll draw up a roster."

A little curt, if you get me. Cool. It's as I've often said: it isn't always advisable to do better than the boss. But either way, the grand Sixth Form support reading scheme was under way.

I was in my room, some fortnight or so later, with Sarah Meacham and a couple of others. We were designing posters for a poetry reading we hoped to put on in a lunch hour. It struck me that we needed a little colour.

"What we want is felt pens," I said. "Can we get any?"

"I could try the ladybird room," said Sarah.

"The... the where? Where's the ladybird room, Sarah?"

"In the tutorial department. It's where we teach the little ones

– the slow readers. They read from those little Ladybird books, you know the ones? Ladybird series."

"Oh, fair enough then." I puzzled. "Isn't that rather patronising?"

"No." She was indignant. "No, it's not. It's just a nice name for them."

"Okay. I'll believe you. How is the reading going anyway?"

"I quite like it. I've got that little boy Jack Rogers. We're reading Jack and the Beanstalk. I think he's keen because it's his name. Yes. It's going O.K."

I was left musing by all that. We react to labels, after all, and my initial reaction had been a twinge of disappointment that maybe Sarah was being a little patronising. But, no, the more I thought of it, the more it didn't seem that way. Never underestimate the maternal instinct in a girl of seventeen. It really did seem, the more I thought of it, like a sobriquet that was warm, gentle and – dare I say it? – pretty. Indeed, if we compared it to a few staff room labels for the slower pupils (and Killer, and several others who weren't ex-grammar school, frequently used the term "Neanderthals") it seemed to have a fair measure of affection.

And so it was that I decided to pay the odd visit to Sarah and her colleagues, and their pupils, in the ladybird room. I wasn't being nosy; I just wanted to see for myself how the support reading was going.

In the period when I called, the atmosphere there was a curiously gentle one. Sarah was, as she'd said, reading to the little boy Rogers, and the only other pair was a heavily bespectacled and painfully shy little girl, reading to the bright and bustling Fiona. To be honest, I'd had my doubts about Fiona. She was very much your thrusting careerist, with university firmly in her sights and (I suspect) a shrewd awareness that someone would be writing a reference for her fairly soon. I had a distinct feeling that Fiona would have calculated a stint of support reading would look quite good on a university application – she'd implied as much when she'd asked me about it originally. Which is not to say that she wouldn't apply herself quite assiduously once she was up in the ladybird room, and that afternoon she was listening quite intently as the little girl in specs stumbled over her reading. Fiona, it seemed, was prepared to ginger the little girl on fairly sharply.

"They... come to the... watter," intoned the little girl.

"No," said Fiona. "It's one *t*. *Water*. *Watter* would be double *t*. *Water*."

"Water. Pe-ter want to... is that *luke*?"

"Not *luke*," said Fiona. "*Look*. I told you before..."

The little girl was looking rather crestfallen. I think the talk of single and double t's was spinning round in her head. I made a mental note to suggest to Fiona some time that she tone down her approach somewhat. And then I went to listen to Sarah and young Rogers.

Sarah was smiling happily as the little boy wrestled with a slightly harder book, but with a fair good humour.

"*Jack began*... What's that word, Sarah? That's hard."

"*Immediately*. Go on. Try it. *Imm-eedi-ate-lee*."

"*Immediately*."

"Good boy."

"*Immediately... to climb the... beanstalk. It was* hard work *pulling him-self upwards from... branch to branch, but Jack was a strong boy.*" The odd word or phrase seemed to get through to his imagination, and he would belt it out.

"Very good, Jack," said Sarah. "Good boy."

"*...and he was... de-ter-mined... to reach the top.*"

"Good boy, that's really good."

Now this was just as I would have hoped that the ladybird

room would be. Jack seemed to be thriving on Sarah's enthusiasm – which, for all my earlier fears, didn't seem at all patronising.

Matters continued, in this fashion into the following term. When I mentioned the support reading to Sarah (and indeed, to most of the others) they seemed very happy about it. It was surprising what the Sixth Formers were managing with some unlikely customers. Jack Rogers, for example, seemed happy to be the feted beanstalk hero before Sarah's admiring gaze, but he was in some ways a rather disturbed little boy and had been known, in staff room parlance, to "do a runner" once or twice – to get on his heels and scarper out of school.

I began to realise after a while that the link with Sarah had developed by now into a genuine bond – a real mutual affection. One Saturday morning in February, I had Sixth Form helpers out in the town's main shopping street collecting for local charities. Around mid-morning I wandered down the street to inspect the troops and, for all Killer's gloomy prognostications about our new school establishing itself very rapidly as a hell-hole, I found it refreshing to see the street dotted with our black uniforms and sky blue ties, and to feel that there was something civilised going on.

Outside Woolworth's, I met Sarah with her collecting tin and was a little surprised to see that young Rogers was with her.

"It was all right for Jack to come as well, was it, sir? He didn't know about it till yesterday, and I thought... it *is* all right, isn't it?"

"I don't see why not. Have you collected a lot, Jack?"

The little boy looked very proud and really, I couldn't but think that Sarah's protective support could do a lot of good to a kid who had very little by way of aptitudes or (as far as I gathered) family support. I left them to it, with Jack holding and rattling the tin and Sarah trying her smile on passers-by. Yes, I thought, it's a nice bond.

Isn't it surprising though, how the expert eye looks on

everything differently? I mentioned that little incident to Webster in the staff room the next Monday and immediately found him disapproving.

"It's all right up to a point, John," he said, "but there are a few angles to watch. Had the boy had his parents' permission, for example? No, I'm not being too critical. But remember that the idea of the support reading scheme is that it's skills-based. We're not running a social club. It was just a little irregular, wasn't it?"

I found this frankly finicky but decided to let the matter go. Just Webster being cantankerous, I reckoned, at someone caring without permission. Which was why it was rather a jolt to hear from the Sixth Form a day or two later that Webster had changed the roster of readers. Young Jack would from now on be reading to Fiona.

Sarah came to see me soon afterwards, looking rather hurt and puzzled. "But what's the reason for changing it, sir? I was getting on well with Jack – and he was improving, really he was. I thought it would be a help to stay with the same person."

I was forced to backtrack a little, to try to speculate on Webster's arguments. "I'm not quite sure of the reason, Sarah. Perhaps Mr Webster feels... well, perhaps it's like doctors and social workers. Not getting too attached to their clients. Do you see?"

She tossed her head, rather nettled. "Is it because I took him with me on Saturday?"

"Not necessarily. I think it's just a matter of changing readers around."

"Yes. I see." She looked crestfallen.

I imagined that Jack would be very put out also, and confirmation of that came rapidly – the next day in fact, when Jack did a miniature runner. I went into the Sixth Form Common Room to see somebody, and found Jack (who was very much out of bounds in being there at all) sitting sulkily next to Sarah. She herself looked very sheepish and embarrassed.

"Mr Roker, can you tell Jack to go back? He says he doesn't like reading to Fiona."

"Come on, Jack. You know you're not supposed to be in this room, don't you?"

He looked down. "Yes, sir."

"Where should you be now? With Fiona?"

"Yes, sir."

"You'll have to go back."

"Don't want to. I don't like her. She's nasty to me. She shouts if I get things wrong, and I don't mean to."

"Suppose I have a word with her. Because remember, if you stay here, you could get Sarah into trouble."

He looked wide-eyed. "Why?"

"Well, people might think she's encouraged you to run in here."

"I don't want to get Sarah in trouble."

"Well, come on then. I'll come back with you."

"Jack," said Sarah, "if you're good and do as you're told, perhaps Mr Roker will try to get the readers changed again."

Thank you, Sarah, I thought. Great. "Come on. Let's go back now, and I'll talk to Mr Webster some time about the readers." Grudgingly, the boy rose to his feet.

It was our ill luck of course that Webster should appear in the Common Room doorway as I was about to lead Fiona's reluctant reader out. What had happened was that Fiona, rightly enough disturbed by her pupil's flying exit, had felt the need to report the matter. The net result was that Webster, finding me, Jack and Sarah in unholy trio, had drawn pretty well the right conclusions. His resultant mental categories featured Jack as a shiftless ne'er-do-well, Sarah as a poisoner of the infant mind, and myself as a very definite accomplice.

To Sarah he said, "I appreciate your enthusiasm, young lady, but I'm sure you'll agree that we must keep to the rule book now and again."

To Jack he said, "Okay, sunshine, on your bike. Back to class. Now."

To me he said later, "I'm speaking from experience now, Mr Roker, dependence is not good in these situations. After all, the girl will be off to college in the summer. What does the boy do then?"

"To be honest, Mr Webster, I suspect Sarah would find her way round that one. But, as the boy sees it, surely he thinks he's being punished for turning out to help on a flag day?"

"I think, Mr Roker, I'll leave the roster as it is. And I'd appreciate it if you'd have a word with the girl and – shall we say? – put her off a little."

What would happen next, I wondered. Should Sarah say to Jack, "We're seeing too much of each other"? Or, "We can't go on meeting like this"? I didn't know. All that happened of course was that Jack sulked through his lessons with Fiona (who came to complain to me once of his truculence), and that Sarah worked patiently with the little girl in glasses. And there for a while the matter rested – until the day of Jack's really big runner.

One lunch time, a week later, word reached me in the staff room, from an amused and cryptic colleague, that possibly Webster could do with my support in the gym. When I got there, it was to see a harassed Webster and an equally harassed little posse of Heads of Year and other senior beings gazing at the wall bars, at the top of which Jack Rogers was perched in an ungainly squat, half in and half out of the window. I was very tempted to ask, "What seems to be the problem?" but Webster forestalled me.

"Roker," he grated. "There are two Inspectors in school today. Also a group of Governors is being shown around. We've got to get this boy down."

"What does he say when you ask him?" I said. I was beginning to enjoy this.

"He's stubborn," said Webster. "Defiant. He just damn well refuses."

"Might I suggest," I said, "that we ask Sarah Meacham to speak to him? He does listen to her."

My message was relayed up-corridor, and, after a pause filled only by the grinding of Webster's teeth, Sarah appeared, tracksuited and just back from a netball practice. From the very outset, she realised that her moment had come – that she now was really calling the shots.

It was suggested that she mount the wall bars and reason with the boy. "Okay," she said, and climbed up to the top window and Jack's hunched form. There followed a gentle, whispered conversation; perhaps it was only my delighted imagination which caused me to think of it as a conspiracy.

After a couple of minutes Sarah's voice floated very sweetly down. "Mr Roker?"

"Yes."

"Jack says, if he comes down and goes back to class, can he come back to reading to me?"

I was enjoying this as much as Sarah was. "I'll have to ask Mr Webster, Sarah. We'll have to think about it very carefully."

Webster uttered a snort that was bordering on the apoplectic. "Roker. Listen. Two of Her Majesty's Inspectorate are in school. Three members of the governing body are being shown around. Our reputation as a new school is in the making. Roker, I care about such things. And Roker," there were tears stifled in his voice "in a very deep and fundamental sense, I do not give a toss who reads to whom in the tutorial room. Promise the two of them what you like, promise them anything, but get... him... down."

"Sarah." My voice too, I like to think, was sweet and fluting. "Sarah. Mr Webster says, yes, it's all right. If Jack comes down now, he can read to you again, and nothing more will be said."

For one awful moment, I thought Sarah was about to ask something like, "How can we be sure?" but mercifully intuition told her that this would be overkill. "Come on, Jack," she said. "Down we go." Jack eased himself out of the window and they scrambled happily down. Webster trusted himself to no more than a visible shudder of aggravation before stalking out, and Sarah said, "Come on, Jack. We've got a lesson at half-past-two."

And of course, I couldn't have left things that afternoon without a short monitoring visit to the ladybird room. Jack was throwing himself into his tale of his hero-self and the beanstalk with some of the relish he'd gained from Sarah's admiration.

"Jack... reached... the top of the beanstalk... safely, but... the ogre..." (again he roared the words out with an undiscriminating enthusiasm) "was close behind him."

He read cheerfully on, through the sudden happiness of a story of dreams and heroes, of mothers hitching up their skirts and running to the hero's assistance, of plunging falls and tumbling villains.

The beanstalk... toppled down... there was a tre-men-dous thud ... and the ogre... was thrown... headlong to the ground.

LIPS

The newspaper is big enough to have a staff canteen and that canteen is part of the real world. And Ros from advertising, who must be all of twenty-two, is part of the real world too. She wears smart business suits and has a slinky bum.

At night-time, in bed, Anthony fantasises and dreams of Ros, and aches with lust. And it's not just that, honestly. Ros is a nice person. She's befriended him somehow and they have coffee every morning, eleven till eleven-fifteen.

His diary, scribbled and re-scribbled in the hour before he goes to bed, sings praise to Ros. He is too embarrassed to dwell upon that slinky bum, but pays such tribute to the lovely curved bow of her mouth. As he writes, Anthony is aware that he is over-writing, but he is living in the real world now, and he feels such lust and love.

Her curved lips crease into a smile. "Been busy?"

"It wasn't too bad this morning. I picked up on a Press release from a theatre company and phoned the director. It built up into quite a nice story."

"Will you be a real reporter one day? Well, sorry, I know you're sort of a reporter now, but… well, it's work experience you're on, isn't it?"

"Yes. It's a fix, in a way, because my uncle's the editor."

"Is he? Mr Edwards? Wow."

"Well, yes. I mean, the school likes us to set up our own work experience in the hols, so... Why are you laughing?"

"Anthony, you're so cute. You said 'hols' or something. Is that 'holidays'?"

"Yes. Sorry. Boarding schools use funny terms sometimes."

"What's it like being in a boarding school?"

"It's all right, but it's a little cramped, in a way. That's why I came down here for the... holidays. Just to get out of that public school, Oxford sort of feeling, and out into the real world."

"Aren't they real in your school then?"

"I'm not sure... Can I tell you something?"

The lips crease gently once again.

"When I've finished university, and it probably will be Oxford, I'd like to go into journalism, but I'd like really to write. Novels and things like that. And I've been reading a lot of Steinbeck... Have you read any of Steinbeck's novels?"

"Nah. I read romances mainly. I did read *Lord of the Flies* for GCSE. But go on, Anthony, tell me about Steinbeck."

"Well, he roughed around a lot. He was a ranch hand and he got round among a lot of people. If you're in public school, you're sheltered."

"I wouldn't have liked it. I'd have missed my Mum and Dad something rotten." Her brow puckers. "You're away from your Mum and Dad now, aren't you? In the holidays?"

"Yes. It's not too bad. I'll be finishing here at the end of next week and I'll see them then for a fortnight. That'll be good."

The lips purse. "It must be funny. You're such a kind boy. I bet your Mum misses you."

That night's diary entry picks up on the lips' every nuance, but he does scribble out the word "rosebud".

"Ros?"

"What is it, Anthony? You look very serious this morning."

"It's just a thought, and if it'll be a bother or an embarrassment, I shan't be offended. Next week is my last week. Well. Could we go out together some evening?"

She giggles, then laughs delight. "Anthony, that's so lovely. That's so sweet." Eyes and lips join in pleasure. "Can I think about it for a day or two? Or… say I let you know tomorrow? Hey. I'll tell you what. I could take you to the Nite Spot on Saturday. And then you really would see the real world." She is now beaming as much as smiling. "I'm just wondering what my boy friend would think about it."

Anthony's mouth is dry. "Does he live locally?"

"He's in the Army. I've promised not to go out with other blokes, but… well, you're different, aren't you? I wouldn't hide anything from him. But if he knew you were… what are you, seventeen? …and in boarding school, it'd probably be all right." The lips and the smile are now rainbow. "I'll let you know tomorrow. I'll have a think."

The next day, no Ros.

The next day again, no Ros.

A harassed news editor.

"Anthony. Sorry to land this one on you, but we're very short-staffed. Could you do an obit for us? It's a delicate thing and I wouldn't normally put a work experience boy on it, but… as I say… we're short. And you're a well-mannered boy. Just be quiet and courteous. We've got a pro forma you can use. Just ask quietly and people are usually very helpful."

"Surely. Where do I go?"

"14 St Helen's Terrace. It's a Mr Walter Stevenson. Poor bugger was only fifty-odd. He was a bit of a local footballer, so see if you can get a little detail on that."

"Mrs Stevenson? I'm sincerely sorry."

"Are you from the paper? Do come in. My daughter's inside." The day is bright sunshine, but the house, with the curtains half-drawn, is cool and shadowed.

"Ros, this is the gentleman from the newspaper. This is my daughter, Ros."

The half-hour there seems unreal. Anthony is aware of their grief and tries to hide his nervousness, to be simple and helpful. He hardly dares look Ros in the face.

The picture gathers. Walter Stevenson was born and bred locally. A jobbing builder. Devoted family man. Leaves to mourn his wife Hilda and his daughter Rosaline.

"Anthony, it was so sudden," says Ros. "He'd had a little heart trouble, but lately he looked so well." She is crying.

Anthony is struggling. The football? Walter played for a number of local clubs as a centre half and for over a decade had been coach to East End. Anthony asks awkwardly, "If this is at all a bother, do please say so, but have you a phone number for the East End secretary? Perhaps the club would want to pay a few words of tribute?"

"Yes, of course. Thank you, Anthony." Ros fetches an address book from the drawer.

Anthony crafts so very carefully. He sculpts and phrases, shapes the tribute. He phones the secretary of East End, who says that the whole club is devastated. Walter was an astute coach and an inspiration to the younger players. His obituary goes to press.

On his way for the bus home, Anthony slips into Smith's for a sympathy card, which he sends to Ros at 14 St Helen's Terrace.

Eleven o'clock. Outside, grey and louring cloud.

"Ros! I didn't expect to see you. Are you all right? Are you managing?"

"Yes. Thank you. I'm starting to cope now."

"I thought you'd be away till Monday."

"I thought I'd come in today, it might help. Mum's a bit better, now the funeral's over. And it's your last day, isn't it?"

"Well… yes. I'm glad I could see you before I left."

"I got you these." She passes over the canteen table an envelope and a small packet. "Anthony. The obituary was so kind…" She is crying just slightly. "I got you a card to say thank you, and a book. I went out to buy it yesterday, in Smith's, and that helped. You told me you liked him. Steinbeck. This is *The Log from…*"

"*…the Sea of Cortez?*"

"Yes. You haven't got it?"

"No, but I've wanted to read it for a while. It's a memoir based around his time in Monterey with… Sorry. I hope you don't feel too awful?"

"No, I'm getting used to it. Have you ever lost anyone close, Anthony?"

"No. An aunt, once. And once, when I was twelve, there was a boy in school who died. That felt very strange, but I was young then."

"I must go, Anthony. I've been told I can go home early. But I wanted to see you. The obituary really did help. And I've written a sort of message inside the book. I hope you don't mind." And she kisses him firmly, gently, on the mouth.

Anthony makes his way to the bus stop, as rain skitters rapidly across Swansea pavements. He clutches the card and the paperback under his windcheater, to carry them both to his aunt's house and to read Ros's messages quietly and alone. Crowding his head is the memory of her kiss. And how kind it felt.

INFIDEL

The autumn sunlight filtered through the trees that straggled down the length of the churchyard before us. The funeral procession in the distance had nothing that was chill or really frightening about it. It was more as if Mr Forsyth, having, so it seemed, gossiped and idled his way through seventy-odd years, smoking indolently and happily by the gate that led out of his front garden, was settling now to sleep. It was as I had expected it might feel. It was because I had expected such a feeling that I had come, eventually deciding, with a trembling sense that there was some comfort here for us both, to bring the little boy.

Michael had been shielded from his mother's funeral three months before. We had moved away quietly, to live for a while with his grandmother, and I had just told him that Mummy wouldn't be coming back now – which was about all I could comprehend myself for the time. Marian's funeral had come abruptly, before the shock was really felt; harsh clods of earth had thumped with dull pointlessness against the coffin, deadening any real feeling for what had happened. And the funeral service had passed half-noticed, leaving me without any sort of ritualised image to contain my memories of what had gone. I don't know quite why I wanted to wander unseen past St Thomas's on the afternoon when Forsyth was being buried. He had had, for Marian and me, a warm quality – a cheerful and lazy flow, nodding happily on the edge of our courting summers, smoking a pipe in his garden when I stopped to talk to him, as I was heading up the adjoining front path to call for Marian. Through two years' courtship, he had watched our goings out and comings in – do they use that phrase in funeral services, I wondered – and had been, in a vague, unobtrusive way, a sort of benevolent guardian angel. So many spring evenings, the wrinkled smile, a slow waft of pipe-smoke. "Going dancing, children?" That's all.

The burial passed very quickly, that autumn afternoon. The words of the service drifted across to us, muted, incomprehensible and soothing. Forsyth, Marian, slow dignified language and a peaceful rest. Trees shading the deep earth from summer and winter. That's all. Some sort of comfort. Then it was over; time to go.

The boy watched the departing group of mourners, still puzzled by my earlier explanation that an old man I had known and liked very much had died and was going to be buried. He didn't say much, all the way through.

"Come on then, Michael. We'll walk on down to the bus station. You can look at the buses then, and we'll go home on the bus." It was a regular walk. I took his hand. We took the path that skirted round beside the churchyard, towards the Parade – rose bushes, tennis courts, bowling green. We'd be passing closer, eventually, to Forsyth's grave.

"Daddy? Why do they bury people when they're dead?"

"It's peaceful and quiet, I suppose."

"Are they sleeping, then?"

"Nobody really knows, I don't think. It just seems as if people get very old and rather tired, and want just to lie and sleep quietly. That's what I'd think."

"Like that old man? Was he very old?"

"Yes, he was quite old."

He stopped, pointed to the fresh grave. "Is it over there, Daddy? Where the old man is."

"Yes. Do you see? They've put flowers around the place."

"Why?"

"Well... I suppose if he is sleeping, it'll be nicer sleeping with flowers around him. They're nice flowers, aren't they?"

"Daddy? Has Mummy got any flowers? Where she's sleeping?"

"Oh, yes, she's got flowers. Granny and I go and put them there."

"When do you?"

"On a Sunday. Come on. We're going down to the Parade now."

He stopped, looked back at the churchyard. "Where is Mummy lying?"

It was on the far side of the churchyard. "Right over there, love. Hidden away by the wall of the church."

"Can we go there? To see the flowers? And to see if she's sleeping?"

"Some other day. We'll have to go now, to get our bus."

"I want to see Mummy. Where she's lying."

I just said quietly, "Come on. Some other day," and steered him gently down the steps to the Parade. "Granny was expecting us for tea at four." He looked hurt and confused. "We'll see if there's anybody playing bowls," I said. We wandered on slowly, silently, past the rose-bushes. A sudden brightening from Michael.

"Daddy?"

"Yes?"

"We could take some of these flowers. And take them up to where Mummy is lying."

"We can't take these, though. They belong to the Council, the people who keep the Parade."

"Can I come with you and Granny? One Sunday?"

"We'll see."

"Why not, Daddy?"

"You're still a little young."

"Why?"

Why? In three months, he'd hardly spoken of his mother. At night, sometimes, I'd heard him sobbing, had gone in to talk to him, talked about everyday things till he settled down. Should he perhaps come, one Sunday? It was helping me, in the way Forsyth's funeral had, to get used to it.

"Perhaps you can, yes."

He smiled eagerly. "And we'll go this Sunday?"

"Yes, I expect so. You and me and Granny." The phrase echoed sharply back in time. Once I would have said, You and me and Mummy. Michael seemed to notice nothing, went on smiling happily.

We cut past the bowling-green then, round behind the Parade, where courting couples go on a Saturday night. Marian and I on summer evenings; later, both of us, with Michael, the walk to the bus station. A known setting, stretching out to the quiet rattle of the bowling-green, the quiet sleep of the old man in St Thomas's.

"Laid to rest... " Yes, rest. It was very quiet there that afternoon. The links, the threads, catching and weaving into the texture of the living town. It was something....

Something for me anyway, a slow, sad attempt to fuse truth and comfort, to realise my new place in the world and to locate Marian within it. Something, for me. And the boy?

"Daddy? Mummy wasn't old."

"She was about my age, Mike."

"Why is she sleeping then? You said only old people wanted to sleep."

"Usually, yes. But sometimes people get very ill. Like Mummy."

"And die?"

"Yes, sometimes."

He was staring wide-eyed at me. "Daddy. You won't die, will you?"

"Don't be silly, Mike. No, I won't die."

"But you could get ill, like Mummy."

"No, I won't. I'm not an ill sort of person."

He looked very worried. "Only ill sorts of people can die?"

"Yes." A lie. Had to be. Marian and I, the agreed shared faith: the simplest and best thing is always to tell a child the truth. The true agnostic upbringing. Criticised, resented, you ought to have him christened, and so on, but we clung to our faith. Marian and me....

He still looked worried. I wanted to say, We'll all see Mummy again one day. Up in the sky or somewhere. God knows.

"Take my hand going down the steps, Mike." We were clambering slowly down into Quay Street, a descent into the warmest part of the town's history, Bristol-trading sea-ships in the past, and commerce now, the town, the past, holding us to what has gone... Vague. I was still looking.

"Daddy? Is God looking after Mummy now?"

"Well, it's difficult to explain. I've told you, haven't I? Some people think the whole world was made by a God but some people don't really know. I don't think we can be sure."

"But God lives in Heaven, doesn't he, Daddy? Miss Rees told me. In school."

"Well. The people who believe in God believe that as well, yes."

"Where's Heaven, Daddy?"

"Well, I don't think anybody knows. But if there was one, it would be a place where people rested after they were dead."

"Is Mummy there?"

"I expect she's resting somewhere, Mike. We'll go on Sunday, shall we? We'll put flowers by the place where she's resting. Would you like that?"

He drove on, earnest and insistent. "Daddy. If she's in Heaven, we'll go there one day. When we're old. Won't we?"

I squeezed his hand. "Surely. I expect we'll all be sleeping together one day. You and me and Mummy. Just like we used to, in our house. Do you remember? After we'd all gone to bed. We'd all sleep together, in the same house." I put an arm around him to lift him down the last few steps. "It'll be like that one day. In that churchyard perhaps, or some sort of Heaven. We don't really know, but it'll be something like that."

He gazed around him sadly.

"Come on, Mike. Let's see if there are any swans on the river today."

We walked over to the railings by the quayside. Two swans were there, one preening his mate gently, the two curving gracefully in a slow, balletic movement.

Mike gazed out, preoccupied. "I expect she's resting."

WHEN THE SUN WENT DOWN

Jumbo and his mother talked quietly about his father, that breakfast time. The pain had eased, and it looked as if things would be all right now, that he would be comfortable again, for two, three weeks, a month perhaps. It went like that: for two, perhaps three days, the pain would be bad, really bad, and they'd need to stay with him in relays, through the night. Then, for a few weeks, it would ease. So it was over now again, for a while. He'd be comfortable again.

Jumbo felt vaguely reassured that there was no reason why he shouldn't go off now to the cricket in Swansea, with Mark and Quentin. His mother was tired, certainly – so was he, for that matter – but she could sleep, there'd be time to sleep now, in the small bedroom next to his father's room, waking quickly if he called now and again. His voice would judder into the rather tense ripple of sleep they'd both learned to cultivate. He felt it was all right about the cricket; the only snag was that strange feeling, an oddly compounded sense of disloyalty and irrelevance, involved in the plunge into a bright August sunshine, while his father lay at home, trembling and ill. Out of the curtained tension of the bedroom into the August splash of sun was too vivid a leap to contemplate for the moment.

His mother looked at him wearily. She smiled. "You go to the cricket, John. He'll be easy again now. I can get a bit of sleep this morning."

"You're sure you can cope?"

"John, come on. We've got to keep things going. You go, if you're not too tired."

The sun was streaming in through the kitchen window. There was still a little early morning haze around. Still, the feeling: there didn't seem much point. His father was ill; two years perhaps to go. Maybe three. And Jumbo was tired. There didn't seem a lot of point in going to a cricket match.

"What time are Mark and Quentin calling?" asked his mother.

"Around half past nine, I think. I said I'd see." He rose slowly and went upstairs to wash and shave and change.

The tarmac drummed and sped beneath the car's tyres, and slowly Jumbo could feel the stirring that always came these days, the day after the pain had gone again. The world stirring back again, back to life.

Quentin was jabbering that morning. The reddish tinge to his beard and to his rather shaggy, semi-curly mane of hair glistened in the sunshine and, all the way from town to Swansea, he was giggling, gesticulating, exuberant. His masculinity always seemed to be threatened by this readiness to giggle, a sudden, girlish silliness at the edge of a flabby strength.

Mark was sleeker, hard, and forever elegant: Zapata moustache, the eyes set deep and dreaming. People often described him as "deep." He was coasting, cruising, in a conversational third gear to Quentin's racing, revving top. Jumbo, burly, pink, close-shaven, solemn, sat crammed into the back seat as the car sped on. Quentin speculated and enthused, mainly on cricket, most of the way to Swansea. Mark nodded, coasted. The car raced on to St Helen's cricket ground.

St Helen's was warm and happy. Jumbo was back now, back in the world and happy. It was beer, occasional pints in the sunshine, sun on their backs as they stripped to the waist, and sat with a pint glass each and a scorecard. They watched the Australian innings build slowly, could gaze relaxedly at the warm and graceful competence of it all, with time, in flickers, to enthuse over the occasional Glamorgan wicket. At such moments, Quentin would bubble momentarily, and buzz with excited advice – "Keep the ball up to him now, boy. Right in the blockhole. Pin him down." Then the match would settle, the Australians would re-assert themselves, and Mark would nod a little distantly. "They'll have three-fifty on the board by the close." Jumbo, plump and faintly shy, his skin peeling even now a little as the sun beat down, sat wondering.

The girls appeared a row or two ahead of them... when? Two o'clock, two thirty. A little after the lunch interval. Jumbo became aware of them by degrees. The blonde was the main one clearly: bright, her blouse crimped and white, buttocks cleanly clasped in tight navy jeans. And there was a dark girl, bronzed, aloof, still wearing a denim jacket, even in that heat. And the quiet one.

Only gradually, it seemed, did Jumbo become aware of the conversation sparking into life between their own bench and that of the girls. It was the sort of conversation, on Quentin's part anyway, which always irritated Jumbo: banal, at times almost simpering, as Quentin's giggly attempts to ingratiate led him too often to the puerile.

"Don't do anything I wouldn't do," said Quentin to the blonde girl, as she left the bench for ice cream. And the girl's reply was as predictable as it was wearying: "That'll give me plenty of scope." But Jumbo felt dazed today, numbed even, and the talk seemed unreal.

The blonde girl went to the ice cream van again, wiggling her fingers in a mock-girlish wave before leaving. Quentin assembled the beer glasses: "I'll get these, boys." He caught up with the blonde, without hurrying too much, at the foot of the terracing. When he got back, Mark merely tilted his head casually in enquiry.

"Disco in the Belgrade," said Quentin. "Top end of Mumbles pier."

In the Belgrade, just before midnight, Jumbo sat alone, drinking Coke. There didn't seem much point in any more beer, even though the bar was still serving. He'd wait now, till Quentin and Mark got back. One o'clock, they'd agreed. The car was parked just up on the main road. He'd been drinking Coke since he'd left the girl, around eleven o'clock. "Tell you what," he'd said, "I'm going to get a Coke. I'll see you again." The hint had been obvious enough; she'd drifted away and Jumbo had wandered off alone to the bar.

So he'd sat for an hour, drinking Coke; so he sat now, as the dance hall emptied. In the end, he was at the table alone. A couple of cleaners were in, and a caretaker. They didn't take much notice of him; nobody seemed too bothered about getting him out.

Only after about a quarter of an hour did the caretaker come up to Jumbo's end of the hall. He gazed for a while at a serving hatch just to one side of the bar. It was wrenched a little way out of true, not off its hinges, but buckled.

"Buggers have mucked this up now," said the caretaker. "Bastards." He wrenched at the door, trying to re-align it, struggling with the weight.

"Want a hand?" asked Jumbo.

"Could you give us a hand, son? It's the hinges. They're out of true. Bastards have wrenched it. If you... can you hold it back?" Jumbo took the pressure against the screwdriver as the caretaker strained to force it back into shape. In the end they had to unscrew half of it, and bend and buckle. They were sweating. "Not ideal," said the caretaker. "But I'm getting it done tonight. Bugger it."

They finished round about one, and Jumbo set off then for the car.

"See you," he said.

"Thanks a lot, son. Cheers."

Quentin was back to the car first, scowling, sulking. Not much to say: "Bloody silly bitch." Mark, when he arrived, just seemed lazier, relaxed. Quentin just growled briefly: "All right?"

"She was all right," said Mark. "No problems."

Then back, the dark and the constant headlights, the journey home into a brooding silence. A sour sort of feeling.

Jumbo was outside his house, almost heading down the garden path, before he noticed the doctor's car. And then it all seemed to blaze because his mother just had the wall lights on, and the house was rather dark.

"He passed away, John, about nine. I didn't try to phone or get in touch. I didn't know where you'd be really. I knew you'd be heading back before long."

There were complications and confusions for a while. The doctor. And then they settled, Jumbo and his mother. For a while, grief, but briefly only; it seemed to pass, and they were musing then. It was on now, deep into the night, with the first suggestions of dawn outside. His mother got the photographs out.

It was the photographs of his father they looked at mainly, a young farmworker before the war, a lance corporal in wartime, then a carpenter, then his own business. Stolid, sturdy. His father and mother. Then the three of them. Dazed, slowly, they leafed through the photographs, not quite taking it in. At last, his mother spoke.

"John. Your father. How I met him. Or before I met him, really." She paused. "It's odd. A funny sort of story. We were in the same Sunday school. It was a big thing then, Sunday school, and the Sunday school trip was a big event. And one year we went to Tenby. I was twelve, twelve or thirteen. And your father was sixteen. Even older maybe. Seventeen." She mused a while. "Yes. There were four years between us. Anyway. We hadn't... I mean, we didn't really know each other then, or talk or anything. And we, that was us, my friends and myself, we played on the beach all afternoon, it was a lovely sunny day. And then later, when the sun was going down, we came up to the top of the beach, where it was sheltered. It was getting cooler then."

There was a long silence. She gazed at one photo. The two of them and 3 Cromie Terrace. "Cromie Terrace, John. You remember. That was our first home."

She seemed to toss her head a little, as if to clear it. "Anyway. We went to the top of the beach. And there was a café there, with little tables outside, looking out over the beach. He was there, your father, on his own." She gazed into the sad little mist of dreams.

"The others, the other boys, they'd gone off. After girls, somebody said. And he'd stayed, on his own, he hadn't wanted to go." Again she gazed at the photograph of that first home. Again she stirred to get back to her story. "And then... then we waved up to him. And... John, do you know? He came down to talk to us. He was four years older, remember. And then... it's a funny thing to remember... he stayed with us till the bus came. He helped us to build sandcastles." Suddenly, again, her eyes were deep with tears, and she was gazing at Jumbo, wide-eyed. "We were just little girls, John. And... and... sandcastles."

She sat, head over her arms on the kitchen table, and wept. Jumbo sat beside her, smoothing the silky greying hair. As he sat he gazed again at the photographs. 3 Cromie Terrace, first home. Lance corporal. Carpenter. The dawn was breaking now, a still pure light on the town roofs that straggled down beneath the kitchen window. He gazed and gazed. The tears were there somewhere, but deep, prickling deep down. He gazed at his dead father with a sense of desperate affinity.

SOUNDS OF THE TOWN

When Archer and big Jess called to see me that evening, they had to park some little way down the road, because of a party next door, and had to walk back. This gave me, gazing furtively out of the front room window, ample opportunity to study this unlikely pair of allies which Fate and the Local Trading Action Committee had brought my way.

Archer was a short, dumpy man, with all of the ponderous self-importance which associated with the phrase "prominent local businessman". Yet he had, perhaps through his habit of thrusting his hands down into his overcoat pockets, something of the bearing of the Chicago mobster. The impression was helped along by the presence at his side of Big Jess: lean, spare, crisp, gum-chewing, wisecracking.

Inevitable also that, when a committee got set up to slog it out with Welsh Finance, the big shots on the Chamber of Trade should ally themselves with the civic society. And Ronnie Archer was that year's Chamber of Trade chairman. Archer had recently bought up a long row of shop premises which had become vacant at the end of Bridge Street and had set up a trading concern called Supermart. Ironically although the prime movers were local men (with the exception of Big Jess, a Cardiff import), the general ambience of the place was thoroughly unlocal, utterly at odds with the market town mood. It was sub-let to a foodstore, a butcher's (run by Archer himself), and various other make-it-on-the-quick boys, with the whole outfit having Archer as proprietor and Big Jess, Mr Get Up and Go, as manager. Anyway. Allies we were, and fighting, in name at least, for the local quality in the town's trading.

I ushered Archer and Big Jess into the front room and we settled, over coffee, to a deliberation on the formal letter of protest I'd drafted for the Welsh Office. Roles were clearly defined. I'd had to write the thing. Jess had to chip in with comments like "Right. The nitty-gritty", and piddle around with things like Sub-Section 2a of the Amenities Act. Archer's function seemed to rest largely in the dissemination of aura; he hoped, I think, by lying back in his armchair, eyes closed, fingertips touching, and head nodding wisely, to confer a Supermart Seal of Approval upon the proceedings.

Later, we worked over another letter I'd drafted for the local Press.

"With the advent of Dyfed in 1974," I'd said, "the people of Pembrokeshire lost the local quality in their local government. All the more need now to make sure we don't lose the local quality in our trading."

"It's a good line," said Archer. "You play on it."

Afterwards when we were chewing the fat a little more generally, he relaxed into something resembling sentiment. "Trading's changed," he said. "The town's changed. I remember the sounds of the town when I was a boy."

This interested me. "What sort of sounds, Mr Archer?" I asked.

His fingertips joined delicately once again. His eyelids drooped a shade. "Sheep being herded down Bridge Street to the mart," he said. "The rattle of milk churns in the early morning." Big Jess glanced at his watch, and Archer, distracted from his reminiscences, seemed ready to go. I cut in.

"That does interest me," I said. ""I'm planning out a sort of radio play. You know, just roughing out an idea. Anyway, it's set in town, Bridge Street mainly, round about 1920. And what I'm short on is a few ideas for sound effects. You couldn't help me out some time?"

Archer gazed at me in mild puzzlement. "Yes. Yes. I dare say I could. In what way, exactly?"

"If I called to see you and you described some of these sounds of the town, as you call them. Gave me a bit of back-ground."

Seeing no catch, he shrugged agreement. "Call in at the office some time. Or give me a ring. I'd be glad to help." Very obviously, an idea struck him. "I'd get an acknowledgment, if the play was produced?"

I was caught off guard. "Well... well, yes. I don't see why not. I hadn't thought that far ahead really. But... yes. It should be quite simple."

He nodded. "Good. Yes. I'll help you out. Call in at the office some time. You could bring a tape recorder and record me. Or I could scratch something out. Yes." And then his interest drifted away and Big Jess had the chance to draw us back to something he'd spotted in Clause 18 of the regulations for public consultation.

The succeeding weeks were frustrating. We had the tangle of the clash with Welsh Finance to attend to which I found increasingly irksome as time went by. I was more interested in my radio play and in the whole idea, for its own sake, of the sounds of the town. In my various contacts with Archer by phone, I tried to pin him down to some definite session at which he could give me the information I wanted, but Archer seemed to have forgotten about it.

Then I met Georgie Harries one afternoon in Bridge Street. White-haired, bubbling, gentle old Georgie. He'd taught me in primary school over twenty years back, and pleased me, on the few occasions we met, by asking about my writing. I'd written my first stories for Georgie, and he was one of the few people I met around town who seemed to feel, with me, that writing was something with a magic and purpose of its own, not just a means to the end of protest-letter propaganda.

"And," he said, his eyes sparkling, "how's the writing going? Anything brewing?"

I smiled, for I could talk to Georgie. "A radio play is the latest thing. It's about Bridge Street just after the First World War. It's still very embryonic." I told him the story of Archer's reluctant collaboration.

Georgie snorted, with a mixture of indignation and amusement.

"Daft," he said. "I was brought up in Bridge Street in the twenties. Of course it had its sounds. And they were magic, boy. And music. Ronnie Archer's tone deaf. You come up to the house this afternoon. I'll tell you about the sounds of the town."

I was at Georgie's house, with my notebook, promptly at half-past two. "Yes," he said. "I was brought up right at the Swan end of Bridge Street. Pretty well opposite where old Archer's Superwhatsit is now." He beamed. "Now then," he said. "Where do you want to start?"

"Archer said something about sheep being driven through the street."

"Of course there were. The mart ground is just across the road. Sheep would come through, and cattle. You'd have hooves clattering, bleating, herdsmen shouting them on. You'd get up to that in the morning on mart days. What else did he mention?"

"Not much. He said something about milk churns."

"Yes. There were milk churns, coming through on the carts, clanking and clattering. And the ironmonger's opposite. There was clanking there too. He used to hang all his buckets and ironware outside the shop." He grinned. "There were goods of all manner coming through and being sold. I remember one milkman in particular. The milkmen all had the same shout. 'Milko!' Just that. 'Milko!' And one of them, I always remember this, had a very frosty voice, cold and chilling in a way. It always struck me, did that, as a little boy."

"Were there other street cries? Besides the milkmen?"

"Lord bless you, boy yes. There were cocklewomen, up from Llangwm very often, selling cockles off their carts. 'Fresh cockles,' they'd shout. 'Fresh cockles.' And chip carts coming through. They'd shout, too. 'All steaming hot.' And one thing again I remember. They used to stable horses in the yard of the Swan. You'd hear the clatter of the hooves on the cobbles, and then the small boys shouting out. 'Hold your horse's head, sir?' They'd get sixpence usually, for holding a horse's head."

"That's marvellous," I said, scribbling.

"There was a lot besides," said Georgie. "There were coal boats unloading on the other side of the river, they'd come up to the Old Bridge in those days. And you'd get the hooters blasting off now and again. And there was a blacksmith's shop behind us, in Holloway. You'd hear the hammering on the anvil. And the smell of burning hooves, if you're interested in smells. But perhaps they can't do smells on the radio." He grinned.

"That's marvellous, Mr Harries," I said. Then I looked over my scribbled notes. "It's odd though, in a way. While I've been drafting the play, I've been thinking of Bridge Street as a strange sort of early century hollow. You know, sleepy and still. And the sounds of the town just dropping, rippling, into a sort of pool of silence. But, as you describe it, it's quite noisy. Or... is 'noisy' the right word? You said something this morning about music."

"It was music. And, damn it all, we had music. Literally. The Salvation Army used to play on the square every Saturday, not just once a year, as now. And the Boys' Brigade bugle band. And there were street singers, beggars, I suppose and gypsies roaming in. And then the sound of fights. But you still get that nowadays."

I closed my notebook happily.

"More tea," said Georgie. We settled to a second cup, as the old man pottered with the tea tray. Then a thought crossed my mind.

"When I asked Archer to help," I said, "he asked if he'd be acknowledged, if the play ever appears. Would you like me to acknowledge you? You've been a tremendous help."

Georgie grinned delight, and wagged his silvery old head. "That's real Ronnie Archer," he said. "Listen boy. You probably don't expect a primary school teacher to quote an Irish dramatist at you, but I will. John Millington Synge. 'All art is a collaboration.' They're your sounds, and mine. Mine this morning, yours now too. Because you wanted to know. Does that answer your question?"

I called to see Archer the next morning, at Supermart. It was low-ceilinged and garish and had a loud-speaker system installed to relay obscure disembodied comments from one end of the building to the other.

Archer liked to refer to his shop as 'a butchery' and was proud of the policy behind the sign at the entrance: 'All Meats Pre-

Packaged.' His meat was all sold on strict supermarket lines, cellophane-wrapped, labelled and priced, and customers circled round with their trolleys. Presumably the cutting and slicing went on offstage somewhere, but no customer in Archer's butchery was to be disconcerted by the sound of a cleaver chunking down on a wooden counter.

"You've come to see the boss?" said Big Jess, in his natty suit and wide tie. "This way." He ushered me into Archer's office, and left us. Archer showed me to a seat, and we read over a Press release I'd brought to check over with him.

Then: "Did you hear me on the radio this morning?" he asked.

"No. I didn't know you were on."

"BBC phoned yesterday. Wanted someone from the committee to give an interview. I meant to warn you. I went on." He fumbled in his desk. "I'll play it to you. I've got a cassette here."

He switched on and we listened to his sonorous declamations.

"The people of Pembrokeshire have already lost the local element in their local government. They don't want now to lose the local element in their trading."

"Good stuff," I said. "Oh, by the way. Talking of radio." I told him of how I'd collected the information I wanted from Georgie Harries. He nodded, his expression a mixture of mild resentment and apathy, with the apathy winning. Shortly afterwards, I left.

On the way out, I met a crisp and thriving Jess, and we stood chatting a while in the main corridor of Supermart. The place was almost silent, eerily so even. Just momentarily, the quietness was clanged into by the rattle and jangle of a cash register behind us.

"Listen," said Jess, with grinning delight. "They're playing our tune."

We separated. Inside Supermart the only noise was of trolleyloads of pre-packaged meat being wheeled out to the car park. It was a relief to get back out into Bridge Street, to be plunged into the chatter, noise and bustle of the street outside.

WHEELERDEALER

We were all about ten years old at the time, and for Eddie and me it was our first real view of Jasper. We had been aware for a few years of this rather odd little boy of our own age in the house at the corner, protected a little by parents who were harmlessly odd and genteel in their ways, and perhaps inclined to regard Eddie and me as coming into the category of "rough boys". We saw Jasper at school, of course, but he had never mixed with us much at weekends, when we went on regular forays to a wooded area nearby we always referred to as "Under the Hills".

And now Jasper's parents seemed to have relented a little and he was allowed to come with us one Saturday morning. It was one of those spring Saturday mornings of boyhood. There was a deep mildness breathing upwards from the earth. We swung a rope over the branch of a tree and were swinging out and away from it, to the far side of a stream just below the tree. If you swung hard enough and far enough you would clear the stream, but if you swung a little too hard you would crash into a thick hedge on the other side. And the shout, exuberant and gleeful, which I will always remember, is that of the ten-year-old Jasper, swinging out delightedly in his new-found freedom: "I say. We mustn't swing out any farther, must we, or someone's going to get the most awful injury."

Now that really was an idiom which was new to Eddie and me. Eddie sniggered a little to himself, before leaning back to me to whisper, "He's a bloody nancy boy." And from that moment, from a two-way joke, whose implications were lost on the three of us anyway, but a joke which soon included Jasper quite readily, it seemed that the three of us were friends.

For years we rambled around Under the Hills every weekend, until, when Jasper was thirteen, his parents decided to send him to public school. This rather accentuated Jasper's grandness and his original flamboyant idiom, but Eddie and I had grown so used to Jasper by now that a shade more eccentricity made little difference. And within a couple of years, his parents' money seemed to have run low, and Jasper was back from boarding school, and with us in the grammar school in town. Even when Eddie left school at sixteen, we all stayed close; for a brief while we established ourselves as a skiffle group. Eddie and I, who used to thrash away more or less adequately on a couple of guitars, had to patronise Jasper a little, since he was remarkably unmusical and was kept in the group as an inept percussionist, scratching feverishly and happily on a wash-board, with thimbles on his fingers.

I suppose we felt Jasper needed to be indulged and protected. Although I grew aware that the school was grooming him for a scholarship to Oxford, this didn't dent Eddie's conviction that blokes like Jasper were to be accepted with good humour rather than envied. Eddie had been working as a van driver with Exchange and Mart for over a year. He had knocked around a bit.

The morning after Jasper's return from his interview at Oxford we had arranged to meet in the snooker club. Eddie and I looked up from our table to see the swagger of Jasper's entry. He was wearing a pair of dark glasses.

"The Oxford don is back, then," said Eddie, who beamed

indulgently upon our eccentric friend before adding, "He looks a right bloody ponce, doesn't he?"

In the event, Jasper did go to Oxford. I went to college in Swansea. Eddie's career blossomed. After his opening foray with Exchange and Mart, he went into business with his uncle, buying and selling, with a stall in the old market on Saturdays and a small shop in Holloway.

There was something of the archetypal Oxford undergraduate about Jasper, certainly, but equally Eddie fitted with assurance into the ways and manner of the wheelerdealer. He was buying and selling the length and breadth of the town and its environs, with a van crammed full of oddments and an ever-ready wallet, stuffed full of greasy fivers, jammed into the back pocket of his jeans. Sometimes on Saturdays I'd sit with Eddie at his market stall, for the sheer pleasure of hearing his sales spiel: "You take it, you leave it, love, I'm a busy man. But that's quality. For you, a quid, but I can't afford to hang around." He seemed to bring sales patter to the level of a minor art form. He projected a delicate sense of inbuilt self-parody. "At a fiver, love, I'm cutting my own throat. But you take it if you want it. I've got to get on."

When Jasper had graduated from Oxford, he returned to town to teach history at the grammar school. I was coming back and fore from Margam Tech at weekends, and saw a little less of him and Eddie. But then I got a job in the tech in town, and the three us still seemed, in a loose and undemanding sort of way, to keep up our friendship.

At about this time Jasper got married. Rather like a conjuror smartly whipping the big prize from a hat, he produced Kirsty, the striking daughter of a Berkshire stockbroker, a girl whom he'd met in Oxford, and who now came to live in town and seemed, with extraordinary ease, to fit very happily into the roughcast social texture of our Western outpost. The one thing I never really knew was what she made of Eddie. But at any rate, her supporting assurance seemed to urge Jasper on to ever greater deeds of social extravagance. He acquired his first sports car, which he drove very fast in his now habitual dark glasses, with his spectacularly attractive young wife at his side.

At about the same time, Eddie started courting Gloria. There was something wistful, innocent and awful about the spectacle of Eddie in love. Gloria worked in the County Offices and this seemed to inspire Eddie with an awe which Jasper's and my degrees never had. Just as Eddie had wholeheartedly become the wheelerdealer, so he now became, equally vigorously, the doting lover.

I remember vividly the evening when he, I and Jasper gathered in the Jack Tar in Burton, just before Jasper's wedding. Eddie produced, for our inspection, a copper etching which I suspect he had dug out of some job lot as a present for Gloria. It was a print of a curious kind of poemy piece of prose called "Desiderata" – you may have seen it – written by God knows whom, and whether artistically or commercially inspired I wouldn't know. "Desiderata" exhorts its hearers to "Go placidly amid the noise and the bustle... Remember, you are a child of the universe, as natural as a tree or the stars..." Later, it talks of love "as perennial as the grass." Proudly, and four or five pints on, Eddie recited all this to the two of us. "I read that to Gloria, boys. I tell her: Glore. You're the child of my universe." He smiled complacently. "She likes compliments like that." Jasper and I could only sit by, a little stunned by the sheer lyrical awfulness of it all.

Gloria had plans for Eddie. After they married, he was taken into business by her father, who ran a linen and fabrics place in Bridge Street. And Eddie wasn't happy. There wasn't room, in the dainty confines of the Bridge Street shop, for sales patter, wallets full of greasy fivers, or tea from chipped mugs. Eddie was sedately dressed, anxious to please certainly, but seemed now vaguely emasculated.

Mercifully, Gloria's father got the message after a while that Eddie wasn't cut out for this new life up-market. Eddie gave us the news in the snooker club that he was being put in charge of what he referred to as "the road business." He would be taking over from a retiring van driver, and would not only collect and deliver, but would deal directly with warehouses, with a free hand to sort out many of the deals himself. Gloria's old man may have been a shade refined for Eddie, but he had a shrewd head for business. He could see the possible cash value of Eddie's persuasive talents. Eddie soon expanded the road business and ran the occasional stall in some of the markets up the line, Carmarthen and Abergavenny. It may have been an eccentric offshoot of the business, but it suited him well enough.

The three of us were digging in now, in our respective niches in town. We would meet in the cricket club, one or two evenings a week. Jasper still retained a deep enthusiasm for cricket from his public school days, even though he had never been much of a player, and he had now taken up umpiring. He had acquired a short and natty white coat, in a new Australian fashion, and would umpire with enormous swagger and, occasionally, and to the members' considerable annoyance, in his perpetual dark glasses. Eddie had, in fact, been a far better player than Jasper or I ever had, and still played the occasional game, usually knocking a few runs.

And so it all ran placidly until one January day about two years ago. I had taken up a writer's residency in Cardiff for a couple of terms, travelling back and fore at the occasional weekend. One night, walking to Cardiff station, I met Eddie, who had parked his van in a nearby car park, so he could feast off egg and chips in Astey's. He had put in most of the day at Abergavenny market and had called in on a Cardiff warehouse on the return journey, to pick up some order. He gave me a lift home.

This was Eddie in full spate now, the fagsmoking desperado on the road. His van rattled westwards, but with the reassuring sense on my part that with blokes like Eddie, vans don't usually break down. He drove with a sort of hardboiled caution, and chattered away happily about his road business. We stopped to feed again in the Road Chef at the end of the motorway, and Eddie insisted on paying, fishing out a fiver from the wallet which was happily back in business in his back pocket. We went on again, with a grinding of gears, and rolled our way home.

It was the following morning that we heard that on the same night, perhaps an hour or so behind us, Jasper and his sports car had been badly smashed up on the St Clears bypass.

Eddie and I called at the hospital the next day. Jasper was in intensive care.

I phoned Kirsty a couple of times and established that Jasper had a couple of fractures which were simple enough in a way. What only seemed to seep through by hints and guesses was that there might well be permanent brain damage. I don't suppose anyone knew for certain, and Kirsty was, almost audibly, staying calm. But gradually I gathered that things were not good.

Then, in April, I heard that Jasper was out of hospital and (so Kirsty said) home, but in a wheelchair. A fortnight later, I finished my residency and set off home. I called the next morning and Kirsty answered the door.

"Thanks for calling, Rookie," she said. Then she added, slowly, in response to a querying look, "Yes. It is bad." She brightened a little too abruptly. "He isn't in at the moment. Eddie's taken him out in his chair."

It turned out that they had gone to the Parade, a small public recreation ground. Kirsty said that Eddie used to take Jasper there most days, because Jasper liked to watch the tennis.

As I went into the Parade I had that curious recollection of the days when we would set up our swing Under the Hills, the sense that there was a strange mildness breathing from the earth. It was a beautiful spring day.

Jasper, in his wheelchair, and accompanied by Eddie, was parked beside one of the public courts, where a couple of youngsters were playing. As I came up to them, I seemed to be included in the group and the conversation automatically. It was customary enough that Eddie should welcome me with little more than a cheerful sarcasm:

"The Poet Laureate is back then." But what was frightening was that Jasper did not seem fully aware of where I had come from or where I had been.

Eddie had his foot resting on the back bar of the wheelchair and was rocking Jasper very gently to and fro. Jasper grinned round at me a little vacantly. Oddly, apropos of nothing, I noticed that he wasn't wearing his dark glasses.

"It's a fearfully poor game," he said. "Fearfully poor."

And there was still that terrible hint of vacancy in his gaze and in his grin.

Eddie beamed at him amiably. "Don't talk so daft, boy. It's a good game. What d'you say, Jasper boy? They're good players."

And, as Jasper grinned round at the two of us, a little vaguely and emptily, Eddie, very gently, went on rocking the wheelchair quietly back and fore, with an affection that was warm, uncluttered and as natural as the grass.

MARIANNE

"Is your mother cool, would you say?"

Julie isn't quite sure why she has asked this. Samantha talks of her mother so regularly and so often that Julie isn't sure there's much more to hear. But the train journey has been a long one and they've read and re-read the copy of *New Musical Express* which is all they've brought with them to read. They are college friends and are travelling down for the weekend to visit Samantha's parents. And Julie, having heard so much of Samantha's mother, is now a little nervous about it.

Samantha relaxes and smiles at the prospect of talking about her mother, Marianne. "My mother's very cool. Do you know, it's funny to think of it, but she and my Dad were courting in the war. They'd had five of us even before the sixties."

"I haven't heard the name Marianne much, before Marianne Faithfull. Does your mother go barefoot?"

"Yes, she does. How did you know that?"

"It's just the way you talk about her. She seems a very Marianne Faithfull, barefoot sort of person."

"Yes, she is. She is cool. You'll like her."

Julie looks at a station sign: Pembrey and Burry Port. There's a Co-op and something called Clynderwen Farmers or something. It all sounds very Welsh. Which is odd. Marianne doesn't sound like a Welsh person. Samantha looks as if she's really looking forward to this weekend. "What's your Mum like, Julie? You don't talk much about her."

"Different from yours, I'd think. My Mum's a bit severe really. Like, strict. When I was in the Sixth Form even, I had to be in by midnight. Hell, Sam, these are the sixties. And really... well. Absolutely no sex outside marriage. In 1968, for God's sake."

Samantha's smile has gone. "What do you mean, Julie?"

"Sorry?"

"You said, no sex outside marriage. Oh hell, Julie. I hope I haven't said anything... I mean, my Mum's faithful. Hell. She's cool, she's fun, but... she and Dad are devoted. And I rely on that."

Julie doesn't know what to say now. "Sorry, Sam. I didn't mean..." She folds the *NME* and looks for a while at the grey stretch of water beside the train.

"Sammy. You're the only Samantha I know of our age. There's younger children with your name, but your Mum must have been very with it, calling you that in the fifties."

Sammy begins to relax again now. "We've all got slightly wild names. Not too wild, but nice. My brothers are Justin and Damian, and the twins are Abigail and Imogen. And then the baby, she's the afterthought, she's five and she's called Crystal."

"That's nice. I wish I had brothers and sisters."

Sammy's brother Justin meets them at the station and Julie is quite startled but quite impressed by the car, a battered-looking Morris 1000, with bits of bad bodywork painted over in purple. "This is Mum's car," says Samantha. "Dad's got a Wolseley. A posh one. Dad's the conformist in the family."

They are then met, in quite a spacious bungalow and its large untidy lounge, by a tall, dark, good-looking woman. At least, Julie thinks she's good-looking, but she's distracted by the bikini which Marianne is wearing. A bikini. God, if Sammy went up to her place... God, her Mum would die before wearing a bikini. Anywhere. Ever. Marianne is wearing the brightest of red lipstick and nail varnish, even on her toes, and many of the stones in her many rings are ruby-shaded.

And there are children everywhere. They're nice too, because Julie has to admit, yes, Marianne is very nice. She's made some iced lemon water for them and that's good, because it's a very hot day and the journey was very sticky. Julie's Mum would have made them a cup of tea. With doilies and chocolate fingers. But Marianne plonks a tray down on a deal table in the kitchen, alongside a pile of newspapers. They talk college, talk courses, as Marianne (who looks like Sammy: pretty, a sort of older version) finds some biscuits in a tin beside the hob.

The little girl, Crystal, is a pretty child. She's wearing a floral print dress, just slightly crumpled, and she's barefoot too. Julie is flustered but she likes it here.

And then Marianne gets up to fetch another jug of lemon and only then does Julie notice... God. Her bikini is very tight and there are tiny puffs of pubic hair pushing out against the soft skin of her thighs. Julie blushes and looks away. God. College is different, being with boys is different (or might be) but... hell. This is Samantha's Mum. Julie supposes her own Mum must have pubic hair, but... Jeepers.

Then Sammy's Dad (whose name is Graham and who's something important in the oil refinery) comes in and he's a little different. It's Saturday and he's in casual clothes, but they're respectable casual: a cotton shirt and slacks. Julie can't imagine him wearing swimming trunks to lunch. He talks to her very kindly; he's nice too, but Julie is still blushing, she can feel it; blushing deeply. A bikini.

The pub and the dance on Saturday night are good, but, do you know, for one crazy moment, Julie wondered if Marianne would come to the dance with them. She didn't of course, but she didn't fuss about what time they got in, and on Sunday morning, when Julie comes down about nine o'clock (Sammy is still asleep), Marianne is sitting at the kitchen table in a fluffy white dressing gown, still barefoot. She makes Julie her black coffee and just chats very gently and quietly, reading odd snippets from the *Observer*, knowing that Julie is tired.

They don't go to church or chapel (Sammy's told her in the past that the family aren't religious) and, before the train at three, they sit round in the lounge, talking. The books are what really strike Julie now, not neat bound editions like her mother's, but a jumble, heaps of them, piled on shelves and around the room. Marianne talks of novels she's read, she really seems to have read loads, and Julie is impressed. She's thought it was mainly students who were supposed to read.

"What sorts of things do you read, Julie?" Marianne just asks this kindly; she's not grilling her.

"Quite a lot of non-fiction really. Being on a politics course."

"Anything good lately?"

"One thing I liked. Well, it was different. Made me think. Germaine Greer. *The Female Eunuch*. Have you read it?"

"Really, I haven't, Julie. I read the reviews and they put me off a little. I thought it might be all a little strident."

Julie isn't quite sure what "strident" means, or not when connected with a book, so she says well, no, it was quite interesting. Women being socially disabled, that sort of thing.

"Are you a feminist, Julie?" (Oh God, please help me, what do I say now?) "No, I'm sorry," Marianne goes on, "I shouldn't put you on the spot. I'll make the effort to read it maybe, before I pontificate. Oh yes, Crystal, yes, you can ask her. Julie, Crystal's got something she's dying to ask you."

And Crystal (who has taken to Julie) wants the older girl to push her on the swing, which takes them up to time for the train. Julie feels relieved but, really, no, the weekend hasn't been bad at all. Marianne is OK.

On leaving, she gives Marianne a small set of place mats, to say thank-you, and a week later gets this letter:

My dear Julie,
It was really very kind of you to give us the place mats. A lovely gift; thank you so much. Do feel welcome here again, absolutely any time. And I really will read The Female Eunuch. *I think sometimes I'm getting a little staid.*

With love, Marianne.

Below this is a row of kisses. Julie wonders about this, until Samantha assures her that, of the hundred and one letters which Marianne will have written that year, to family, friends and acquaintances, all will have signed off, "With love, Marianne" and been underlined with kisses.

* * *

Nearly thirty years earlier, Marianne had gone to the fair with her friend Jean. And Jean had been irritated by Marianne, if perhaps just a little impressed. Marianne did swank so – and she was wearing all her rings and bracelets. All the way round the fair, she was trying to win bits of jewellery on the stalls. Everything, roll the balls, rifles, coconuts. (Marianne was quite strong for a girl and for fourteen and she'd knocked a coconut right off its stand. And then she'd swapped the coconut with Gilly Morgan for a brooch which Gilly had won). She won a couple of prizes and had a bangle and a ring to add to her collection, which she kept in her bedroom. It was cheap jewellery, Jean supposed, but still jewellery, and Marianne's Mum didn't mind her wearing it; Jean was envious. Marianne wore lipstick too sometimes; her Mum didn't seem to mind even that. Jean's Mum felt that fourteen was too young for lipstick and trinkets. She called jewellery "trinkets".

They wandered round the fair and tried the Dodgems and the Swirls and everything. But Marianne's mind seemed to be wandering. She'd toss her head and hold her hand, with its rings, over the bar of the Dodgem car and God, that annoyed Jean. God. Marianne did love herself. It was too many films: Ginger Rogers and film stars and people like that. God, Marianne did think she was somebody.

Jean bet that Marianne was still thinking of that Graham Rees. He was so old. He was eighteen, for Heaven's sake, too old for them. And everybody said there was a war coming and Graham might have to go into the Army and fight, so what good would that be? Nobody would want a boy friend who was away at the war. And he wouldn't want to be her boy friend, would he? Eighteen? God, Marianne was daft.

Everything annoyed Jean that night. They'd come to the fair the year before, just the two of them, like it had always been, and they'd had fun. And now Marianne was all rings and trinkets and was tossing her head. And Jean knew what was coming next.

Round the corner, just off the main fairground and into Hill

Street, there were these tatty sort of stalls, and some sold cheap jewellery and ornaments (Marianne bought another brooch there) and then there were stupid things. The Bearded Lady and The World's Fattest Man. Jean and Marianne had never bothered with any of that. But, in the middle of all the silly stuff, there'd always been a fortune teller, in this scabby old tent, with just this gloomy old man outside, collecting threepences to go in. There was a plain sign over the tent: *Madame Crystal, Palmist and Fortune Teller*. And that's where Marianne would want to go now, Jean knew it. Just to see what this stupid old woman might say about her and Graham.

And Jean was right. Marianne shuffled about outside the tent. "Coming in?"

"No, I won't bother."

So Marianne gave her threepence to the man, who didn't look as if he could care one way or the other, and she went in.

Madame Crystal looked old and sort of spooky, and the tent inside was dark and spooky too, apart from the one light, in a sort of bowl, in front of Madame Crystal. She was all wrapped up in shawls and veils and things, which looked, in the half-light, as if they might be red. Her voice though was warm and soft. "Give me your hand, my dear. Let me feel your palm." Slowly she turned Marianne's hand around, then took the other hand, gazing at the rings and bangles.

"Are you a G, my dear? You've got a G on your signet ring."

"No, I'm an M. Marianne. G is somebody else."

Madame Crystal seemed to muse. "It's strange. The letter G is speaking to me tonight. Whispering to me. I think that the letter G will play a big part in your life, my dear."

Marianne trembled.

"I see so much for you, my dear. Somebody tall…" (she pressed and fondled Marianne's palm) "…now I'm trying to picture this person. Is he fair maybe?' Marianne was trembling violently. "I think he is fair. He's tall and fair. Tall and fair and not quite a stranger. I think that his life will be linked to yours, my dear. You'll be very close. I see a lifetime together. With lots and lots of children."

"How was she?" asked Jean, as Marianne came out.

"She was okay," said Marianne. "Quite interesting really."

* * *

Samantha is seated, hunched a little over an ash tray, in the smokers' top deck of the service station. She is waiting apprehensively (almost thinking "Please don't leave me") for Marianne to come back from the ladies' room.

The sight of her walking across to her is comforting and Samantha reflects that her mother, now in her mid-fifties, is still a very attractive woman. She is tall and her dark hair which, as far as Samantha knows, she's never dyed, is flecked only slightly with grey. She still wears the deep red lipstick and nail varnish she's always loved and has surely been making up again in the ladies' room. For she's spruce and nice to look at as she comes back to Samantha's table. Samantha moves to go, but…

"No, finish your cigarette, Sammy."

Marianne sits and smiles. Samantha inhales deeply and nervously.

"Do you smoke many nowadays?"

"Now, yes. Just since I started to get suspicious about Mike and his affair. Before that I'd cut right back, I was smoking one or two a day."

Marianne looks at her sadly. "For the next week, fortnight, you do as you choose, Sammy. Smoke, sleep, crash out, what you like. Talk to me and your father. We'll sort something out." She looks straight at Samantha. "Mike's a bastard though. That really was a shitty thing to do."

"I thought you liked him, Mum. You used to."

"Sure, I used to. I used to think he was kind and caring. But he's hurt you and you're my baby."

"Mum, I'm thirty-one."

"And you've never had children. Or you'd know. At times like this, you're my child." And, as Samantha grinds out her cigarette, "Come on, Sam. Let's drive back. Your father'll be anxious about us."

They walk back to the car park, passing the shop's newspaper headlines which speculate on a possible first woman Prime Minister. Then Marianne suddenly gives a start, almost as if frightened.

"What's the matter, Mum?"

"Sorry, Sam. It's such a silly thing. I caught myself out." Suddenly there are tears welling in her eyes. "It's not the first time it's happened today, but we passed the shop then and I was just going to ask if you wanted any sweets. Sort of 'make it better'. And you're thirty-one. Sorry."

In deference, Samantha waits as Marianne blinks back the tears and they've reached the car.

The car is a Rover, Graham's car, to get Marianne up to Samantha's and back a bit more quickly. Graham would have driven, but has sprained an ankle and will be waiting for them now, anxious and upset. They settle into the seats and Marianne edges the headlights into the misty dark and on to the dual carriageway.

After four, five miles, Marianne stirs to speak again. "You're right though, Sam. I did like Mike. And I thought he'd be faithful and constant. All those things. I've got them and I wanted them for you. More than jobs or anything like that."

"Even children?"

"Even children, I think. Oh, I'm sorry, Sam... I didn't mean it quite that way. I've loved you all dearly, but..."

"I know."

Another three, four miles, then Samantha asks, "I'm sure I shouldn't ask this but... just asking. What would you do if Dad were ever unfaithful?"

For a moment, Marianne gazes intently at the road, giving a little left-hand tweak to keep the car out of the path of an overtaking truck which is throwing up spray.

"Can I just tell you something, Sam?" She keeps gazing ahead. "Your father's four years older than me, you know that. But when I first knew him, I was fourteen and he was eighteen. And I loved him then, I really did. I set my cap at him and waited. He went into the Army when he was twenty and I nearly broke my heart. Because I'd barely spoken to him at that stage, and then... I just hung in there, as they say nowadays. And when I was seventeen, and he was on leave, his sister introduced us and... there we were. Away we went. We married two years later."

"That's a lovely story, Mum."

"There's more to it, darling. This is a real strange thing, but it's odd how it's always affected me." Her eyes are still moist. "Just before the war, when I'd just got to know your father, or got to know of him really, well, I went to the fair with my friend Jean. And I went to a fortune teller. Madame Crystal. She told my future. I was a gullible little thing and I swallowed the lot. The tall, fair stranger I'd marry, and masses of children. Oh sure, it was codswallop. But I remember what I felt like as I came away from

Madame Crystal. I knew then, I was certain, I know I was only fourteen, but I was quite, quite certain that I loved your father and that nothing would ever keep us apart or separate us."

For the first time in months, Samantha feels suddenly and deeply happy. "Mum, you've never told me that before. But what a wonderful story." She smiles across at Marianne, who is smiling too. "But the fortune teller, you said she was Madame Crystal. So… our Crystal. Did you name her after the fortune teller?"

"Oh of course I did. I was so proud. God. Six children and all of them strong and beautiful. And Crystal, you'll have gathered, she was an afterthought. So I just felt, okay, I've done it all now. So let's dedicate this last one to the fortune teller in the fair."

Samantha reaches out her hand and squeezes her mother's knee. "So I suppose, when I asked, what would you do – if Dad was unfaithful – it was a silly question, wasn't it?"

"Sammy, I've just occasionally wondered. And what I know, I'm sure of it, is that I'd get round it. I'd find excuses for him. I'd forgive him. I'd take him back. I know that."

Samantha is puzzled. "But Mum, with me and Mike, it's as if you've been saying I should leave him."

Marianne's momentary surge of happiness seems to die back a little now. "I've tried all along, darling, not to tell you what to do. But… yes, I have wished you'd leave him."

"But why? If you'd forgive Dad?"

"Because Mike's a bastard. And you're my baby and he's hurt you."

* * *

Samantha is not to know that five years earlier her father had gone one lunch time to a fashionable West End restaurant with the young woman who'd been his secretary for the two years he'd been posted to Head Office.

Becky, the woman, was dainty and bespectacled. For most of a very good meal, she and Graham toyed with their food. They were both quiet – morose even – in Becky's case sullen, and they said little that wasn't desultory chat. Only eventually, after the pudding had arrived, did Becky broach the subject.

"So you'll go back to the earth mother then? And that's it?"

"Obviously, I'll go back to Marianne. Didn't you always know I would?"

"I think I did, yes. I've known that for two years, I think." She looked down. "I tried to pretend you wouldn't, that you and I would be something together. But I think I knew." She stirred and prodded aimlessly at a profiterole. "So can we communicate? Can I just write to you?"

He looked startled. "I'm sure it would be better not, Becky. We have had a good time, but it's best left now. And your letters arriving… it might just stir it all up again."

Becky gazed at him curiously and suddenly flushed brightly. "Graham, I'm sorry. 'Stir it all up again'?" She looked quite breathless. "You haven't told her?"

"I decided to. Maybe it was the coward's way out, to impose that on her. I suppose I should have kept it to myself. But that's not the way Marianne and I have ever been. We've always shared everything."

"But Graham, this is ridiculous. For God's sake. What are you supposed to have done? What did you tell her you'd done… we'd done?" Graham stayed silent. "Graham, you've given me a lovely time and I've enjoyed it. You've wined me and dined me and we've been to theatres. But we've never consummated it. And you know, you've always known, I was ready for it, I wanted it, and you stayed so cool and aloof at the final moment and you'd kiss me good night. God, I had a bath running once, and you didn't want to know. So what have you got to tell your fertility goddess? God, Graham, you've got nothing to declare."

"In a way, no. It's a sort of semantic thing, isn't it? When is an affair not an affair? There were feelings involved, Becky. I did... part of me loved you a little..."

Stiffly (she looked deeply hurt): "Thank you so much."

They were both uncomfortably aware now that this was a restaurant which wouldn't expect scenes. They waited, quietly, as the coffee was set out.

Graham stirred sugar slowly. "Becky, I was just very, very fond of you. I wanted to take you out, go places.'

"And at weekends, back to Wales. It must have been good. Wild sex, maybe?"

Graham said nothing and, after a moment, Becky whispered, "I'm sorry. That was a little uncivilised." She spooned cream around the top of her coffee, neatly and carefully. "This is a silly thing to ask you just now, but... with... Marianne... what did you see in me?"

"Becky, I've told you. I liked you. I was very, very fond of you. And..." (he was looking a little angry now, but with whom it would have been hard to say) "perhaps it was all a relief. The civilised restaurants. The theatres. And you're elegant. All that, after the... the... my marriage has been like a high tide, really. A rollercoaster. Does that make sense?"

She dabbed a little cream very gently away from her pastel lipstick. "I suppose I should get up and walk out now, Graham, and say, I'll leave you to pay the bill. But then you always have paid the bills and... I am grateful. I'm hurt, it's hurting now, but it was a lovely experience." Stiffly, she stood up. He rose, went to her side and they shook hands. "Best of luck with your marriage."

Graham's train was due out of Paddington later that afternoon and he had time to potter briefly in Covent Garden (somewhere he liked, that Marianne liked, and where he'd never been with Becky). He didn't re-read Marianne's letter until his train was out of Paddington.

My dear Graham,
I haven't replied for two days, I know, because it's all been such a shock. I am getting used to it now. For the moment, I'm clinging to the fact that, as you say, the friendship wasn't consummated and I'll hold on to that, I think. I do trust you on that and believe you. I'll always believe you. And no, I'm not going to haggle and negotiate and be too bloody awful – although I'll probably roast you a few times. But we've got to get ourselves back together. We've been too much together for this to spoil it. Please hurry back.

With love, Marianne.
P.S. As you know, at this point I normally throw in a row of kisses. But this seems too serious a letter for that. So I'll just say again:

With love, Marianne.

* * *

It is a burgeoning May day, a wonderful sunny afternoon, as Jacqui parks her car, collects her case from the back seat and walks into the gloom and heat of the nursing home. She makes her way down to the nurses' room. Cheryl is there.

"Hello, Jacqui. Coffee?"

"Thanks. Who have you got for me today?"

"Marianne today. Just the one. We're trying to ration some of the others a little – sorry – but Marianne does so enjoy having her hair done."

"Her hair's still very strong and springy, Cheryl. It'll always take another trim."

They sip coffee. "Is Marianne made up ready?"

"Susie's making her up now. We don't give her lipstick every day now, but she insists on it for your visits. Funny thing is, she mixes us up sometimes, but she always remembers you."

"I think she likes the occasion. Being made pretty. I bet she was a good looker once," Jacqui ponders. "She often mentions a Graham. Was that her husband?"

"Her husband, yes. He died about two years ago."

"So what age is Marianne?"

"Not that old really. Mid-seventies. But the dementia set in years ago. From what I gather, her husband did wonders with her, keeping her at home to the very end. A very caring man, I believe. And then he died very suddenly, so nursing home it had to be."

"Shame. But… how bad is it? She sometimes seems quite clear."

"In some ways, yes, she's clear, but it doesn't always connect. And she can never remember if her husband's alive or dead. And it doesn't seem to worry her. It's funny. In her own world she seems a very happy person."

They finish their coffee and Jacqui goes up to Marianne's room, where the old lady, tall, rather good-looking, and with strong silvery hair, is wearing her bright red lipstick (which she's smudged just a little) and several of her rings.

"Hello, Marianne. Those are nice rings."

"They're my rubies, my dear. Aren't they nice? I've always loved rubies."

The May sunlight glints for a second or two on Jacqui's scissors as she starts to snip edges. 'It's a lovely sunny day, isn't it, my dear? What month is it?"

"It's May, Marianne. A lovely May day."

"I thought so. I love May." She casts a sly look up at the hairdresser. "Shall I tell you a story?"

"You always tell me stories, Marianne. What story have you got for me today?"

"It's a May story. A May story." Marianne sounds quite triumphant. "Years ago, my dear... it's Jacqui, isn't it? Well, years ago, Jacqui, I went to the May Fair. With my friend Jean. And we met a gypsy. Can you believe that? A gypsy called Madame Crystal." She pauses and blinks. "I think she came to live with us later. She was my daughter, I think."

"So did the gypsy tell your fortune, Marianne?"

"She did more than that. She cast a spell on us. On me and Graham. I'd gone to the fair with Graham, you see. Or it may have been with my friend Jean. But the spell she cast was on me and Graham." She pauses, she is quite immobile for a few seconds. "Is Graham still alive, do you know?"

"I think he died, Marianne. About two years ago."

"I thought he had. But it doesn't matter, because the gypsy had cast her spell on us and we had such a happy time. It wasn't just a spell, you see, it was a good luck charm. And we had lots and lots of good luck and lots and lots of children. Have you ever met my children, Jacqui?"

"I met one of them the last time I called, Marianne. She was your daughter Imogen. They call on you very regularly."

"They do, they do. You're right." She gazes at Jacqui solemnly. "How many children have I got, Jacqui, do you know?"

"Six children, I think. I'm not quite sure."

Marianne seems content now and basks awhile in the sunshine as Jacqui's trimmer works round her neck. Then she suddenly gets startled, a little agitated.

"Oh my dear, I'm so sorry. I was telling you a story. What was it about?"

"It was about the gypsy. Madame Crystal. She cast a spell on you and Graham."

"Yes, of course. Silly of me. Well, now then." And suddenly a rather sly, even wicked look comes into her eyes and she stares at Jacqui intently. "Well, I'll tell you what happened next. A wicked witch came down, from a foreign country. From England. And she tried to tempt Graham away. Wasn't that an awful thing to do?"

"That was terrible, Marianne."

"But my dear, it didn't work. Because Graham and I were charmed. We were both under Madame Crystal's spell. And the wicked witch had to go away. There." And she seems to relax now and sounds satisfied. "I believe in gypsies, my dear. Don't you?"

Jacqui smiles and nods agreement. "That was a lovely story, Marianne." And Marianne does not respond; she may even be asleep. Time passes quietly as Jacqui's trimmer purrs gently at the base of Marianne's neck.

The May sunlight breaks in brightly and reflects off the stone in one of Marianne's rings, so that Jacqui is suddenly dazzled. She blinks and has to put her trimmer down for a second to brush away a sudden, unexpected moisture in her eye.

●

NIGHTINGALE

The Swansea campus had changed by the time I went back there on a course some years after leaving. It was swollen by then, plush-upholstered and obese, so different from the bright days of my youth.

Then, like an eager young wolf cub, I had feasted off sliced bread and cigarettes in an Uplands flat, to prowl out, down Bryn Road on warm spring evenings, headed for scruffy hops in common rooms, and sniffing the salt air slapping against the dirty beach along the Mumbles road.

Now I was older, calmer (happier, yes), living for the time being in my parents' home, eating and sleeping well, I thought of the painful magnificence of that time. Sometimes I stirred in the middle of my steady eight hours' sleep a night and wondered if, as things were, I should ever become middle-aged, if there was a risk in being comfortable. I thought of the times I had shuffled out, grey and unshaven, with the morning light, to the cigarette machine in the Uplands, to add to the sharpness of my youthful stomach a further edge of mild indigestion.

It had all been a bit much. Child of the early 60's though I was, I couldn't really have gone on living like that. We had had keen appetites, which lit our dreams and dealings with the sharp colour of expectancy and hope, and shot them through also with the quality of real pain. We had had our own bright cosmopolis: Chinese restaurants, French films, American paperbacks with the £.s.d. stickers torn off to make it look as though they'd been bought in America. We were wild creatures of the new metropolitan world and had searched frantically for basic loves in the happy frenzy of our big-town life.

I would end so many evenings like some sort of impossible beautiful-dreamer from an American film, playing the piano in a deserted pool-room at two in the morning, while the evening's perfumes faded, the pall of cigarette smoke grew thicker, and the music slowly died away. Either that, or walking home from Killay after a polite good-knight kiss from a nice little bank-clerk. Nice girls were more my line, when all's said and done.

Which brought me, of course, to the parental home in Haverfordwest and a steady job teaching history in a local grammar school. It made sense. If I married one of the prominent local nice girls, I could settle down and sublimate my wilder flights of erotic fancy in marital union. It might have made me middle-aged, but a continuation of my student life would have blown the top of my head off by the time I was 25.

I was well into my 20's, the school had sent me on a three-day course to Swansea, and I met Louise Nightingale again.

I had emerged from one session of the course, overwhelmed and gloomy, at mid-morning on the last day, to walk away from the smell of plush leather, down the drive to the Mumbles road, to catch again the smell of salt air to see if it was the same. Louise, in jeans and duffel-coat as of old, small, bright and smiling enigmatically, was walking up the drive. She had been the craziest and the loveliest girl friend I had had in Swansea. It hadn't lasted very long and I had never known what to make of her. But Jim, who worked now in the College Registry, said she always asked about me.

"Geoff," she said. "How lovely to see you. What are you doing here?"

"I'm lost, Louise. Whatever happened to 1961?"

"I know. Isn't it hideous? I'm hoping to get away as soon as I can now. It's no fun here any more."

We stood for a moment, before she smiled and took my elbow, turning me back towards College House.

"Come on, then. Let's talk over the last few years. We'll have some coffee in one of these new snack bars. You're not married or anything?"

"Not even anything."

"Good. I can still flirt with you. Come on, lovely." Louise seemed not at all surprised that I was teaching in my home town, and smiled inscrutably. She had worked for a few years without much success or inclination at a PhD, getting by on grants, research assistantships and part-time teaching at a local tech. She was ready to get out now and had an interview for a job as an extra-mural tutor. Then she grinned with a surprised pleasure.

"Geoff! You're from Haverfordwest."

"Yes."

"That's where my interview is. It's an informal one. Any time in the next week or so. When are you going back?"

"Tonight. Six o'clock train."

"Are you? Lovely. I'll come as well. I'll phone this man and he can fix me up. Morgan. Organising tutor for Pembrokeshire. Do you know him?"

"I've heard the name, that's all." But I was too bemused with this beautiful good fortune to bother about organising tutors.

"What's Haverfordwest like, Geoff? Oh, I must go. Prof expected me at eleven. I'll see you at the station. Quarter to six? Tell me about it on the train. And perhaps I'll get the job and I can come and flirt with you every night. See you."

The down train. It is quarter to six of a lovely April evening and I wait outside High Street station, ashamed of my new meritocrat's brief-case, hunching my poetic soul against a snack-vending machine, watching buses with poetic names: Oystermouth, Langland Bay, Caswell Bay, redolent of frustrated No 85 journeys back from beach dances to the Uplands. Louise, bright, breathless and late, scurrying past thundering city wheels to meet me. Grinning. "Okay?"

She is surprised at the humble and very small nature of our train, so I tell her of this branch line, avoiding like hell the superior clichés about backwaters, expressing my love for small ramshackle train journeys into the quietness of West Wales.

"We go past Llanelli and into little Carmarthenshire villages. Like Ferryside. It's on Carmarthen Bay and there's a curious grey stretch of water wandering beside the railway for a long time. Then we change at Carmarthen and we'll have an old style corridor train, very old, very dusty and beaten-up. And around through all the farming villages in Pembrokeshire, Whitland, Clynderwen, Clarbeston Road. It's a lovely run."

Louise is pleased. "And what about Haverfordwest? Is that a farming town?"

Slow shuffly sort of rattle and we're headed for Llanelli. A quiet blurred mingling of accents from a few seats around us, soft West Walian lilts, the occasional broad agricultural Pembrokeshire dialect. Music when soft voices quicken.

"It is a farming town, really, yes. It's a commercial centre, basically, but it's agricultural, round about. The mart day is still a big day and you still get cow dung tramped out into the street, so all the bank managers and building societies and all of those boys can't get too much of a smooth hold."

She smiles. "Please don't stop. I like hearing you talk." She takes out some cigarettes, an American brand, and throws the packet on to the table between us. "Help yourself."

I shall. I shall smoke many cigarettes this evening and parcel up my dreams and wisdom, roll them across the table to Louise. We dream a little, watch the blue wisps of smoke, the sudden mild noise of Llanelli. On again, out into the country now.

Louise looks straight at me suddenly, a faint frown between the eyes, wondering. "Didn't you want an academic career, Geoff?"

Lovely question to be asked – implies I could have had one.

"No. I wanted to wander round a bit and write. I had a sort of Steinbeck wandering-ranch-hand mood about me."

"I know. You told me once. Have you written?"

"A little." Uneasy. I have planned and schemed so much. One day. I'll make a story out of you all, your West Wales voices on shabby little trains, you too, perhaps, Louise.

She smiles at my silence. "What did you do? After you graduated?"

"I worked on a bread round for a while. But that's a lie, or an exaggeration. It was more of an extended vacation job, really, only till the end of October. Then I started teaching halfway through a term, and the next September I was in my present job. Very orthodox. I have a brief-case, as you see."

Smile. "It's rather sweet. Suits you."

We smile and smoke and talk, watching little places like Kidwelly, and talking of Swansea, impossibly avant-garde pieces of my fiction and Louise's poems, remembering (on my part) some confused evenings when I never quite knew what she really thought of it all.

Then a wheezing, a slowing down and a crackling loud-speaker voice: "Carmarthen, Carmarthen."

"Come on. We change here. We'll get some tea and crisps."

I take her hold-all and my brief-case, help her down from the train. We are left holding hands. A deep, sweet moment at seven o'clock of an easy April evening, nuzzling together queuing for tea and crisps, bought from a trolley pushed by an old man who munches a biscuit between toothless gums.

Louise has a black coffee, which I too used to drink, getting slight indigestion from it often. We lean on the wall outside the buffet to eat these crisps, she, still in jeans and duffel coat, cheerfully disreputable, I a little ashamed of my schoolmaster's outfit, wishing the brief-case to hell out of there.

Our second train arrives and I can show her this scruffy old train in which, at least, I can take some personal pride. A faded, once-grand compartment, with mirrors and a map of the Western Region on the wall, all to ourselves.

Here we huddle. Here she slips her hand through my arm. Here I know the quiet delight of taking this girl through the very scenes and amiably shabby wanderings of my dreams. Out of Carmarthen, and an hour or so to go.

She looks at me with enquiry. "Do you like being a teacher? Or do you call yourself a schoolmaster?"

Worth pondering, this distinction. "Depends on my mood. If I'm status-seeking, 'schoolmaster', certainly. It carries weight; shows I have a BA and teach 'A' level. Sometimes 'teacher'. If

I'm in one of my ranch-hand moods – it suits those better. There's a tougher, more practical sound to it."

"So a 'teacher', tonight?" Startles me, for a minute. She's perceptive in these things.

"Yes."

"And do you like the job?"

"Yes. At least, not just the job. I like the whole life, all of it. It's solid. They're young faces, belonging to the town, and I've got something definite to work on with them. And even if I muck it up, which I do sometimes, the whole job is something which the town accepts, so I'm a real, living part of the town."

"Your town?" Is she making fun of me? No, she squeezes my arm happily and smiles. "Go on, Geoff. I told you. I like hearing you talk."

"Yes, my town. If I'd gone anywhere else, or been an academic in Reading or Sussex or somewhere, I'd just have visited it for holidays, and never really been part of it again. I want to write about it, catch its moods." Dare I add: I want a partner, a woman, to share my dreams, read my scraps and jottings of small-town living? Not yet, not yet. Use a bit of sense.

Louise still gazes towards me, very intent. "Were you happy at Swansea? With the sort of student life we had there?"

"Very much so, in many ways. I often look back and wonder if I've lost anything now that those days are behind me. I've gained, certainly."

"You're calmer, happier." I look with enquiry. She nods. "You're more articulate, more yourself. You were slightly frenzied in those days."

"Is frenzy so very bad?"

"Perhaps not. Well, I don't know about frenzy. Eagerness, maybe."

"Eagerness." She's right. "We were eager then," I ask, "weren't we, all of us?" Quiet, smiling nod. "We wanted to see everything, question everything, try it all on for size. But look at some of them now. Hell, Louise, I don't want to get fat and lazy."

She laughs. "You won't, Geoff. Good God." She looks out of the window. "What station was that?"

"Clarbeston Road. We're just about into town."

"Do you know Gwyn Morgan? The man who's interviewing me? No, you said you just knew the name. He said he'd meet me at the station."

Well, damn and hell, what now, confusion, I wanted to walk Louise now – my Nightingale – round the quiet bowling green on the Parade, it's only eight. Damn these officious buggers. Hell, we're there.

Scramble off the train, nearly drop the bloody brief-case in my annoyance. Big, dark, hairy organising tutor. "Have you met...?" and similar crap. Christ, she knows him.

Then a big arm of hairy Morgan's round Louise's waist. "Come on, lovely."

"Cheerio, then, Geoff. I'll see you. It's been a lovely trip."

So.

Hell.

Sod it.

To walk, then, slowly, from the station and to ponder this kick in the emotional groin. I had wanted again the stirring of the adolescent prowls of my student youth. So I got it.

Walk through Cartlett, Salutation Square. Breathe in the savour, always fresh, of this, my town. Yes, I'm articulate now, and I'll calm down. Some people busy, hurrying, most more lazy, sauntering, as I cross the New Bridge and stop to watch the river flowing quietly, as ever, through the lazy grey streets of this, my kingdom. I was not born for thee, immortal bird. She will drink black coffee and smoke now till the early hours. That sort of thing always did give me indigestion.

AN APRIL STORY

She is so obviously the classic innocent, a brown sepia image, the type and representative of all our yesterdays. But let us fill the empty spaces, gather her coming century around her, build a fiction.

Haverfordwest, Market Street, 1906. The print, a sepia photograph, has been on my wall for some time. Superficially, it is pastoral. There is no vehicle to be seen, save for a horse and cart at the top end of the street. Foreground, a cluster of small boys and bigger boys standing with caps and breeches, hands in pockets, feigning a nonchalance towards the camera which they are still eyeing furtively. And right up foreground is a girl of perhaps fourteen, with a broad-brimmed hat, a bright white blouse, spruce black stockings, a shopping basket and a skirt whose hem is just slightly uneven. She gazes at the camera much more firmly and intently than the boys.

Large Victorian (and older) buildings frame our view. Commerce House, a department store, stands massively behind the girl. A shoe shop has a jumble of its wares hung outside it. And halfway up the street is Brigstocke's printing works, already publishing a weekly newspaper. It is a busy town. But in a way of course they are innocent – innocent of two world wars, of Fascism and international Communism, of Thatcherism and the Internet.

The little girl, foreground. What are her hopes and expectations? Let us say she is fourteen, that her name is Louise and that the month is April. It makes good sense to say it could be April, for it is bright enough to take a photograph, yet cool enough for the boys to be dressed warmly. But, for Louise's sake and for the sake of her story, let it certainly be April. She is coming into life and leaf and April is a good month for setting out.

She gazes quite intently at the camera, arms wrapped around her shopping basket's handle, almost in a pose. There is no smile, but I suspect she is pleased to be caught thus by the camera and for her image to be preserved. She would hardly imagine though that the writer of this present memoir will gaze upon her and her Market Street with such fascination, in ninety-three years' time.

Let us move rapidly now to fiction. She is a little stern in her expression, not just because of the camera, but because Benny the butcher's boy has bothered her again. Every Saturday morning, as she goes to Market Street for her mother's shopping, she is chivvied and annoyed by Benny, who delivers on Saturday morning for a High Street butcher. He will sneak up behind her and tweak and tug the long black tresses of her hair. Once he tried to kiss her. The other girls say he likes her and this morning she feels the mingling of a hot exasperation and an excitement which isn't quite driven out by the excitement of the camera. Despite this she is sedate and ladylike. In time, she will marry Benny the butcher's boy, Ben Butch. For a year, he will be sent away to Swansea to work with a butcher-uncle and to learn his trade, while she works in a draper's shop. She will wait for him and they will marry in the spring of 1914.

It is going into February 1916 and Ben Butch has been in France now, with the Welsh Regiment, for over a year. He has been back just once, on a short sick leave, because of frostbite in his feet – they call it "trench foot". His is not a bad case, but Louise was horrified to see the puckering and to sense his pain. And then he recovered and returned to the front.

She is lonely. While Ben is away, she is living with her parents and can only hope for that one day when he comes back and they will set up home together. For all that, there are still things to do and, occasionally, places to go. She still has her job in the draper's shop and a little money, but ekes it out spending a little on clothes and on trips to the picture palace. She goes regularly to Bethesda chapel, where there will be a social next Thursday and the Annual Tea and Concert in March. Last Sunday the pastor gave what seemed to have been an important sermon (for the local newspaper reported it at length) on "God's Trust in Man", but Louise's mind was half-attending; filling her thoughts was the prospect of a new production at the picture palace. A play, a real play, not a picture, with eighteen artists, a play called *The Broken Rosary*. She will love it. The glitter and the escape.

Some things she can only dream about. There will be the dance soon at the Assembly Rooms, where the dancing will not start till eight and there will be dancing and cards till the early hours. But that will be for the gentry really, and anyway it will cost two-and-six.

She contributes though (and this is her one very earnest, if rather timid contribution to the war effort) to the local cigarette fund, so that her pennies, her threepences and the occasional sixpence will help towards packets of cigarettes to be sent to the boys at the front. She reads in the newspaper of how grateful the boys are. "My chums and I settled down to a really grand smoke," said one, and she is pleased to have donated something. Ben Butch smokes. Perhaps some of her contributions will make their way to him.

The newspaper is sometimes a worry though. She reads of the deaths of local boys, of amputation, and the dreaded "trench foot". But their spirits are high – only sometimes Louise is uneasy about how high their spirits are. One local soldier (whom again she read about in the newspaper – the paper is so full of war news) was sent back on sick leave with damaged eyesight, but just said that a shell had exploded "unpleasantly near". She is frightened by the heartiness and afraid for them. Afraid for Ben Butch – and for herself.

One edition of the newspaper had a strange story of a senior army officer who is being court martialled at Scoveston fort for drunkenness. Louise just wonders what all the fuss is about. There is drunkenness in town every night.

Remember: this is a fiction, Louise's April story. So I could tell you now that Louise will hear, later that year, that Ben Butch has been killed in action. He will have died a brave death and been a credit to his regiment.

But our story will not tell you that. This writer wants happiness for Louise and was moved and touched by the sense of hope and radiance which emanated from her in 1906. So Benny Butch will live. He will return, he will set up home with Louise just after Christmas 1918, and their two sons, Gareth and Robert, will be born in 1919 and 1922.

The nineteen-twenties are wonderful. Ben Butch is back home, one of the lucky ones, unscathed save for a bad limp, and by 1926 he has set up his own butcher's shop in Bridge Street. The four of them live over the shop.

The twenties, going on into the thirties, are the era of Louise's young motherhood and she is glad that she and her sons have Bridge Street and the town, with all their noise and excitement. Rising elegantly at the end of the street is the Swan Hotel, a coaching inn, which has a yard where horses are stabled. There is the clatter of hooves every morning and the older boys run after the horses, asking if they can hold a horse's head for the farmers who clatter in. Louise will always remember the day when Gareth, her elder boy, rushes home, flushed and excited, to announce that he has just held a horse's head. Louise loves such things. She mothers the boys with humour and humanity.

The nineteen-thirties are a mellow time. Ben's business does well and they are earning enough now to send the boys to the grammar school, where both do well. In 1937, Gareth will leave town for the teacher training college in Cheltenham. Twice, the rest of the family go up to visit him and Louise is intrigued by the vista of such a large and gracious town. Otherwise, they travel very little; their holidays are to Tenby or the Gower coast.

There is plenty in town which they enjoy. Not only is there the Palace Cinema now, but the new County Theatre at which, on one memorable night, soon after the theatre has opened, they hear a performance by Paul Robeson. Louise has never met or seen a Negro before and has an excited sense that the town is moving now to some greater familiarity with the world beyond. They go to the pictures very often; Louise would love to go to dances too, but this cannot be because of the legacy of Ben's trench foot.

Louise's first sight of Adolf Hitler is on a newsreel at the Palace and she watches later newsreels with the same mixture of disbelief and amusement. He seems a comic foreigner, a Charlie Chaplin figure, jabbering and gesticulating, and she cannot take seriously those people who talk of the threat of another war. In time however, she feels a little knot of tension tightening in her stomach. Surely, it cannot happen again. Surely not. When she sees on the Palace screen the picture of Mr Chamberlain, returned from Munich and his talks with Herr Hitler, waving his paper and saying it is "peace in our time", Louise is exultant. She clutches tightly to Ben's arm in the darkened cinema and is literally weeping tears of joy. She feels she could not have faced another war. Then come the annexation of the Sudetanland and the march into Poland — then war. Louise is numbed with disbelief. First Gareth and then Robert are called up.

Louise finds war even harder the second time around. She has Ben Butch beside her now, which makes for comfort, but at night sometimes she can feel him twisting and muttering in his sleep and she knows that he, like her, is plagued by dreams of two sons overseas and at war. Gareth is on a minesweeper; Robert in the infantry.

Life goes on of course, but the daily round of the butcher's shop is not the pleasure it was in peacetime. There is rationing for one thing and they are often beset by customers who would hope for more than their fair share, who would hope that Ben could somehow conjure a little extra. They earn less of course, but Louise doesn't care about that. Her mind is on her two boys, overseas. Letters arrive from them occasionally, but they are an odd mixture of the laconic and the jolly and Louise doesn't really trust them. The action had been "pretty hellish", Gareth said once, but "the boys are bearing up pretty well". Louise is afraid of censorship, afraid that something awful has happened (or will happen) to her sons. And yet she knows that, like everyone else, she must be cheerful and get on with things and be proud of the fact that her sons are serving their country. Never before has she wished she'd had daughters, but she sometimes wishes that now. Yet nothing will erase the constant recollection of her two sons, so far away, so young.

The war at home is cruel too, on times. There are air raid sirens, with their eerie wail; there is heavy bombing in Swansea and, once, in Pembroke Dock. But all the time it is her sons' plight which leaves Louise most frightened.

She and Ben go to the Palace and the County still, they love the cinema, even though the trudge to get there through the blacked-out streets is rather sad. Lately they've seen Errol Flynn in *Virginia City* and James Cagney with Pat O'Brien in *Boy Meets Girl*. Louise has grown to love American things and still cherishes the recollection of hearing Robeson sing, even though she never has been (and never will go) to America. There are dances still, run by the dairy students, the Home Guard, all manner of people, and you can get in for two or three shillings. She would so love to go and feels that dancing might really help to lift her spirits, but with Ben's trench foot that is impossible. Once though, they do go to a dance, run by the Home Guard, in which Ben is a corporal. He and Louise go along and she can dance with his friends. It's not the same as dancing with Ben would be, but she still finds the music and the movement a kind of comfort.

Louise could hear, in 1943 or 1944, that either or both of her sons is missing, presumed dead. But this fiction will not do that to her. It is clear of course, given the manifold cruelties of her and our century, that such a thing could happen. But it will not. Gareth and Robert will survive. This is partly charity. This writer has come by now to admire Louise's resilience and decency, has grown indeed very fond of her, and wishes for her a happy outcome.

VE Night is ecstatic. The streets are thronged and lit again, there are cheering and singing which last until the early morning.

Louise and Ben both get very drunk, something they're not really used to, and Louise is sick on the way home. But it just doesn't matter. She knows now, is sure, her sons will soon be back and safe.

We move into the post-war world. Mr Churchill warns of an Iron Curtain coming down over Europe, and the first atomic bombs have been exploded in Hiroshima and Nagasaki. In the euphoria of the boys' return, Louise barely notices.

But now? As we move on, Louise becomes ever more shadowy and enigmatic, the strands of her story more difficult to gather. What will she know and feel and experience?

She will have what are sometimes known, with either sentiment or derision, as the simple things in life: a husband and two sons who have survived the two Great Wars; good health; grandmotherhood, robust and roseate. She will never travel to America but she has savoured so much of what is about her: the moment when her elder son came home to boast of how he had held a horse's head and been given sixpence; fairs and festivals and roasting chestnuts; the smell of bread from cake shops; thronged streets, hot Christmases, the returning warmth of spring. Our April story wants all that for her, not because it seeks to be sentimental or unreal, but because this fiction is suffused with the feeling that the simplest lives, if allowed to carry through, unimpeded and unbereaved, can indeed be magical.

The little girl gazes out, sedate, inscrutable, from her photograph of 1906.

BIRTHDAYS

The row blazes across a hundred and fifty miles of motorway and two service stations. It is as if a strip of neon has been laid beneath the blue ribbon of motorway in the atlas and a thin line of red light has blazed its way Eastwards from the Carmarthenshire border to the south of Oxfordshire.

"There's no way, I'm telling you, am I making a bloody speech."

"But Father's expecting it. He'll be disappointed."

"Disappointed, my arse. It'll bounce off his conceit."

"But what harm would be done? It's just a short tribute."

"Tribute, my arse. I owe that guy nothing."

Later, as passions rise: "I owe that man sweet sod all. What a patronising bastard. And he'll have one bloody sycophant after another lined up to pay tribute."

"It wouldn't cost you anything, Mick."

"It would cost me my bloody conscience. The place will be heaving with arse lickers. Let him pay his own bastard tribute."

And finally, as the car tyres snarl across the gravel in front of the house, Nancy snaps:

"Sod you then. Just sod off and leave me. Just get the hell out of it. I'll tell him you've got flu or something."

"Right. Good. I'll pick you up on Boxing Day."

"Like hell you will. I'll come home on the bloody train."

Nancy takes her own suitcase and walks up the gravel driveway.

For a while Mick drives round aimlessly, first as far as the Oxford ring road, until he realises it is the day before Christmas Eve and the traffic will be clogged. He heads back to the village, for no good reason, and finds, as he parks, that the one pub is opening. He buys a pint of lager and sips.

He gazes over a local newspaper which someone has left lying on the bar. He reads of a dispute over councillors' expenses and of a game between Oxford United and Swansea City. He is not particularly interested in the affairs of Swansea City, near whom he lives; still less is he interested in the affairs of Oxford United. But the game is being talked about by the three locals camped in the bar and they show a mild interest in the fact that he is Welsh. Generally though, the evening drifts, until Mick remembers he will need to find somewhere for the night. The regulars look dubious.

"Nowhere in the village, only the widow woman. You'd do best to go on to Abingdon."

Mick is aware he has drunk enough lager to take him well over the breathalyser limit.

"Who's the widow woman?"

"Widow woman. Ah." They snigger. "She'll look after you, I dare say. But she has got a couple of rooms there. Acorn Guest House."

"So that's where?"

"Out of here, left, up the street thirty yards. The widow'll look after you."

The widow woman is his age maybe, mid-fifties, with quite striking dark hair and what is called a full figure. She is very welcoming.

"I'm Brigid. Yes, I've got two rooms and neither of them let tonight."

She offers to carry his suitcase up to the bedroom, then precedes him as he carries it up himself. She spreads the door wide, displays an adequate bedroom, pats the bed. "You'll be comfortable there, I'm sure. I'll leave you to settle in. I'll be downstairs if you want me. We have just the small private bar for residents. It's just you and me tonight."

Later, at Brigid's bar, he drinks more lager and she sips a port and lemon. "Travelling far?" she asks.

"Just hanging round really," he says. He is getting drunk now, but at least he is aware that he is getting drunk.

"Married man, are you?"

"To tell you the truth, I've dropped my wife off at her father's. It's his birthday tomorrow."

"And weren't you invited? That's a strange thing."

"To be honest, I was invited. And I un-invited myself. Lot of family nonsense. I'll show you this." He produces the invitation and reads it to the woman. "A Celebration of the 70th Birthday of Professor Emeritus Justin C Barclay. Poet, Philosopher and Human Being."

"Holy God, that's a clever man. So didn't you want to go?"

"It's because of all that that I didn't want to go. That card. Crap. He had them printed himself, I think. Probably wrote it himself."

"One little thing. It says he's a human being. Now isn't that a strange thing to say?"

Mick stares hard at Brigid. "That is the strange thing to say. Or the pretentious thing. That's what got to me in the end. All of Daddy-in-law's greatness and then "human being". I am a very humble man, says Daddy-in-law. A dreadful man, Brigid. May I call you Brigid?"

"Have you and your wife been married long?"

"For thirty years, Brigid. Thirty years. Her name's Nancy. She's a sweet girl. But there's a funny side to all this... well, not funny, it's sad now really. But we'll have been married thirty years on Boxing Day. Thirty years. And our anniversary... we call it our birthday. That's a personal thing. And shall I tell you what? Not for twenty-five years has that old bastard, Professor Emeritus, Daddy-in-law, remembered our bloody anniversary. And we'd have been up there now, from December the twenty-third through to Boxing Day, glorifying his bloody birthday, and not once would it have been mentioned. Our birthday."

"I hear what you're saying, Mick. He sounds a hard man. I'm sure you did right to stay away."

After she has gone to her bedroom, Brigid strips, quite sumptuously. She cradles her heavy breasts in her large red hands and gazes at her naked form in the mirror. She slips on a night gown and lies on the bed, her light still on. She hears Mick's steps in the corridor outside and her legs part slightly. He goes on to the bathroom, where he pisses noisily. She lies, with the light on, until she falls asleep.

In the morning, Brigid informs him a little stiffly that she is closed over Christmas Day and Boxing Day. He heads for Abingdon and finds a hotel into which he books for two nights. On Christmas Eve, he looks briefly at Abingdon's shops and has just the odd lunchtime drink before going into Oxford for the afternoon.

He spends Christmas Day in the hotel in Abingdon with the two married couples who are staying there, Len and Mary and their friends Ron and Cynthia, from Barnsley. They go there every year, now the young uns have flown the nest. They are solicitous towards Mick, who reluctantly has his temporary separation drawn from him by Mary's probings. After Christmas dinner, Len performs card tricks for two hours. In the evening Mary and Cynthia take out their holiday snaps.

But Christmas Day has its redeeming sub-text. In a world in which it might seem there is no hope, there is the hope embedded in Mick's trip to Oxford on Christmas Eve. There he found a florist, an Interflora dealer, who will deliver for him first thing on Boxing Day. It is fortunate that Mick once practised calligraphy, for he was able to squeeze quite a long message on to quite a small card. It ran: *The whole family contains only one human being and she's lovely. Our birthday is on Boxing Day. See you at the lodge at twelve.*

As Nancy reaches the lodge on Boxing Day, she is stumbling with the weight of her suitcase. Mick pushes it aside and gives her a big, frustrated hug.

"How was it?" he asks.

"Awful," she says. "Shit awful. That doesn't make you right. But it was shit awful".

They drive off through a closing and enclosing afternoon, back to the motorway. They talk of other things, past Christmases, past birthdays, the children, whose silly idea it was to get married on Boxing Day anyway. Radio 2 whispers love songs from the 60s and 70s and they listen, as Nancy's fingers drum out the rhythm on the dashboard. And then, somewhere between the Severn Crossing turn-off and the Magor service station, they hear the voice of Billie Jo Spears, singing of her blanket on the ground. It is a talisman. Nancy just says, "Our birthday, Mick."

Now they are hastening to get home. There is little traffic and the car is racing through the dark. Nancy beats time to Radio 2, humming a little under her breath, her fingers drumming on the dashboard. "Hurry, Mick, hurry. Hurry on home."

OUR FATHER

A sad old man, that white and frosted Boxing Day morning. Happy, deeply, that my daughter Liz was in love and would be married soon. But also sad, watching the gentle white fields of my boyhood gleaming in the winter sunlight and feeling that a very delicate, very profound way, of living and loving, was fading from the world at that year's end.

The bitterness of the rather nasty conversation I'd just had with my son Sam was still sour in my mouth, but it wasn't only that. He was a clever boy, Sam, writing a PhD, but there were so many clever boys around these days. They could come, all of them, to the lovely pale green sweep of the woods at the village's edge and still think the place was a backwater. They would look upon our little church, when they came home for Christmas, and lash out angrily at it all, at the ritual, the ceremony and the peace. That morning I wanted to look out over the fields, hard by the churchyard, let the tears run down my face, and remember it all, treasure it, before it had all gone.

They had been so much, our church and our village. They could take our emotions, our experience, wild and violent, could distance them in simple ritualised scenes, contain them in familiar ceremonies. They could take our very lives and place them in a perspective which we could understand. I tried telling Sam once that the church and the community were like literature in that, but he wouldn't listen.

Sam objected to ritual. And how could I explain? It had meant so much. The real things in life, the big, deep things, birth and love and death, we have to ritualise them and enact them if we are to understand. We have a christening dress and a bridal gown and a shroud. And so we clothe our most profound emotions and experiences for our own self-expression, give them voice and form. Only something as irrational as ritual could sustain the beauty of that kind of experience. But how could I have told Sam that?

He had been half-drunk that morning, sardonic, bludgeoning, a little aggressive. He'd been swaying slightly, standing in front of the fire and we'd argued, as always, with tolerance but with no real understanding.

He'd snorted irritably. "Rubbish! All of it."

"What's rubbish, Sam?"

"This wedding of Liz and Tony's. All the toppers and tails, the buttonholes, the organ playing, here comes the bride. Christ!"

"Come off it, Sam. It means a lot to them. It expresses something for them."

"Pity. I wish it didn't. No, I mean that, Dad, I really do. I'd think more of Liz and Tony, I really would, if they'd get married in a register office. Just scrap the ceremony, sign on the dotted line. Just say: We want to join in a particular socio-economic relationship. Now give us the licence and let's go."

"Socio-economic relationship, be damned. Have a heart, Sam. You'll fall in love yourself one day and you might want more than a licence to satisfy you then."

He'd laughed and hiccuped slightly. "Oh, God, am I getting drunk again? Why do I always get drunk when I come home for

Christmas? And so bloody sour?" He'd smiled at me bleakly. "I must feel for you all, you know, I mean that. I always end up wanting to change you."

I'd offered him another drink, and he'd taken a small one. "What do you want to change about us, Sam?" I'd asked.

"All of it, damn near. The church, the village life, the school. Good God, Dad, you've been head of that school for over twenty years. The archetypal father-figure. It's all so corny and so boring."

"I really have enjoyed it."

"Sure, sure. But I suppose there are just times when I wish you'd do something completely reckless, like taking a job in another area. I don't know. Oh, and the church-going bit. Are you really a Christian, Dad? Really convinced? Intellectually?"

"I think I respond more and more with my feelings as I get older, Sam. It means a lot to me."

He'd been at least half-drunk by that time. He'd lurched a little and pointed at me.

"I'll tell you one thing, now. One thing you could do. To make a young man very happy."

"What's that, Sam?"

"When you go... well, you know, you'll die some day. When you go, I'd like to see you go without any ceremony at all." He'd been pointing and emphasising every word. "No ceremony. A quick cremation and that's that. I'd really admire that."

I hadn't felt angry at that, just sad and hurt. "I'll be buried in the churchyard here, Sam. You know that."

"Sure. Sure."

Then Liz and Tony came in and Sam had beckoned them over for a drink. "Come on over. We were talking about rituals."

"Oh, lovely," Liz had said. "Someone's told you. Tony and I

are getting married. You'll have all the ritual you want then."

Liz had been easy and happy and smiling. Perhaps she'd underestimated how aggressive and rude Sam could get in these moods. She was used to Sam anyway and didn't often take offence. But as the conversation had rambled on, about the wedding ritual, I'd begun to get uneasy. It had all come out eventually. We'd all known of course, but it was the first time anybody had said it openly.

Sam had been holding sway. "Okay, it's a ritual. And you like rituals. Fine. But look at the symbolism. What does it all mean? White dress. The symbol of chastity, the giving up of virginity. Well, bloody hell, Liz, you're pregnant!"

The whole mood had gone really sour then and Sam had known he'd gone too far. Liz and Tony had walked out. There'd been no scene; she'd said something about making tea and they'd gone out. We were all used to Sam.

"There was no need for that, was there?" I'd said, after they'd gone. "That was just bloody-mindedness."

"Okay, I'm sorry. The big loud-mouth. The man they can't gag or something. But I get like that, Dad, every time I'm home. I want to knock everything down. I get mad. It's all so bloody dishonest."

"Oh, Lord, Sam, what's dishonest?"

"This wedding. Hell, if a girl must symbolise her silly bloody virginity – and who cares anyway? – well then, let her wear a pretty little white dress. But Liz isn't a virgin. Not that I mind that. I couldn't care less. But why pretend?"

I thought perhaps I could explain, because I could feel it all, but all the facts and the common sense had muddled me, so I'd come out into the lovely clear morning, to stand by the churchyard and dream.

I could see the fields and they were frosty green and peaceful.

There, in the autumn perhaps Liz and Tony had made love, innocent and eager for each other, and she'd become pregnant. Now she wanted something to express this giving of herself. Sam could use words, he was the articulate one. He'd sit by the hour, I didn't doubt, by the electric fire in his London flat, and rationalise his love affairs. But I was sure he didn't know the happiness that Liz had known.

Of course she wanted a white dress now. Time didn't matter. Facts, the order of things, didn't matter. We'd all understand.

The churchyard and its elms were old and wise. It all meant so much and I was sad to know that it must all pass away soon. But my grandchild would be born in the summer, a boy perhaps. Would he, an old man too, stand here, look at the fields and feel what I felt then? Conceived out there, could he conceive all this?

***

My father died last week. A mad, ugly winter, train lurching home, and what sense does that make, Dad's dead, he's gone. The train heaving, dislocated and crazy, over sickening, spinning rails. A sick, sick, journey.

I stood by the graveside, pale and ill, and was amazed that Liz looked so calm. Peaceful. But she'd been the one who was close to him. So crazy. Mad.

Listen to the service. "Thy servant..." There's no bloody sense in that. There's nobody listening. I was ill and wretched, wanting to call to those old trees to lean over and shelter him, keep him safe, look after him, poor Dad... But that didn't make sense.

Liz was calm. Moved, sad, very, very sad, but she wasn't sick and lost as I was. In the end she took my arm. "Come on, Sam. Let's go home." And I walked out of the old churchyard. She was so sad, was Liz, but she could take it.

Tony took her arm then. "If it's a boy, we'll call him Henry. He'd have liked that." Liz nodded, tears on her face.

"Call him Henry." That I do not understand. I wish to God I could.

THE PATH TO PORTHGAIN

We were just setting out on our walk. We'd cut down the back road behind the Bishop's Palace on to Whitesands beach and it was just as we strode briskly on to the coast path through to Abereiddy that she said it. "You should try writing. Try a short story."

"Do you find it therapeutic?" I asked.

"Oh yes. I mean, I don't write autobiography or confessional or anything. But stances and attitudes creep in. Very obliquely sometimes. But you've been hurt. See how a story works for you."

Over the previous few weeks, I'd told Cheryl a little about my divorce and I'd heard a lot about Arthur, her husband. Again, that morning, I felt that maybe she wanted to talk, so, as we squatted on the grass overlooking the Blue Lagoon just beyond Abereiddy, I asked again.

"Are things with your husband so bad?"

She tossed the untidy mid-brown hair back from her eyes and her full mouth smiled. She took my hand. "You met him that one Friday, didn't you? What did you feel?"

I was wary. "He seemed a little aloof, maybe."

"He's patronising. His attitude... it's archetypal. The little woman is indulging herself in weekend watercolour courses, so he wearily drives her down to St Davids, as a favour. And he patronises you, I'm sure. But you're a real watercolourist, you're a minor celebrity."

"Aren't you a minor celebrity too? You've published all those stories."

"Arthur thinks business world, he thinks money. Publications and watercolours don't come into it. Come on, let's walk on." Again, the smile, the full firm mouth. "Where did you say we were having lunch?"

"There's a pub in Porthgain. A mile and a half, two miles on."

The Sloop had tables outside and we nestled there after lunch, over halves of cider. "You should write," said Cheryl. "You've taught me so much about painting. Now let me see you writing stories."

I took her hand again and leaned towards her. Her kiss was very chaste and quiet but it lingered.

* * *

I'm sorry. I do apologise. I've misled you – and more than that, I've misrepresented people. Arthur most certainly, and Cheryl in a rather more subtle way, but just as perniciously.

For this, you see, is my first attempt at a short story. I did indeed take the idea from Cheryl, for she is broadly as I have described her. Indeed, the facts of the situation (the summer school, the walk to Porthgain, her appearance certainly) are as I have described them. I wasn't going to be oblique. I was going to write unpurged autobiography.

The feeling I began with was fresh and heady: the keyboard, the pristine sheets in the tray in readiness. And my first few paragraphs, as you have them, eased accurately and pleasantly into the events I have known these last few weeks. The conversation about writing and therapy did take place. Then came the first conversation about Arthur, and I began, even then, to tamper with the truth.

The real betrayal, the stab in the back (and you will see, from the tone of all this that I have yet to learn the writer's ability to separate the fiction from our everyday wish to see justice done) came with my description of Arthur, with my reporting on a conversation that simply never happened. For I've met Arthur a couple of times, when he's driven Cheryl down to St Davids or collected her. And he seems a thoroughly decent sort of bloke. Once the three of us even had a drink together in the Grove. Maybe, just maybe, he patronises Cheryl a little (just enough to fuel my fiction maybe?) but my account of him, those accusations which I've fed into Cheryl's speeches, don't hold up. I think of it now and I think of what I've contemplated with another man's wife and I feel a shit. My hour and a quarter on the keyboard has convinced me of that at any rate. I've fabricated my story maybe, but then it is just that: a story. I suspect I've been fabricating a lot more.

So I must tell you now about my wife. Julie. I shall tell it carefully to myself and try, this time, to be truthful.

* * *

These were the seventies and we were seventeen. We had music, clothes and a strange new freedom. But Julie and I had the coast as well, felt blessed by that rambling coast path that took us through, the first time we went out together, from Whitesands to Porthgain. Back in school, we were outsiders, if ever there were such. We were liked well enough, but she was nicknamed "Mouse" and I "Goggles" and we felt shy and constrained, even in each other's company, when, in the corridors and in the school yard, we stumbled over the first steps of a friendship. Somehow, one Friday, I muttered out my request, "Shall we go out together tomorrow?"

She blushed, but her voice was even. "Yes, we should. Where would be nice?"

"One of the pubs?"

Still she was even-toned. "Is that what we want? Where would be somewhere for us?"

"Do you walk a lot? On the coast path?"

"You know quite well I do."

"Well, let's go out in the daytime. We don't have to go out at night-time."

"Yes, I'd like that. Where shall we walk?"

"To Porthgain?"

"Yes. There's a pub there too, so we'd be there by lunch time. We could have a drink before coming back. Even the squares would approve of that."

"The squares" was a nickname we'd devised, along with a batch of individual names, for practically everybody else in our Sixth Form. As I said, we'd talked a lot, in the school yard and at lunch times. Perhaps we were simply daunted by the boozing and the bravado; we preferred at that time each other's quiet company. So our first date (if anyone, "the squares" or whoever else, wanted to call it a date) was to be a walk along the coast path from Whitesands to Porthgain. It was July.

Julie, "Mouse", had tousled mid-brown hair and rather full lips, but I thought her very pretty. I still do and always have. The composure she'd seemed to collect from the moment I'd asked her out was still about her when we met in Cathedral Close that Saturday morning. I felt bold and happy. We talked of walks we'd made. Both our sets of parents were keen walkers and yes, I'd known when I'd asked her that she walked the coast, because our families had crossed paths many times.

We left soon after eight, cutting down to the Bishop's Palace and along the back road to Whitesands, then up and along the coast. I thought of taking her hand but soon after we left Cathedral Close she took mine. Away from the school, the bluster, the bums-and-tits jokes, she was relaxed. Along the road, from the Palace to Whitesands, we told each other cheerful jokes about the squares. A year's enforced subjugation eased away.

Along the stretch of coast from Whitesands to Abereiddy, we had to walk in single file a good part of the way. She led. Then down into Abereiddy; it was now eleven, or half-past, and we walked very slowly across the beach, side by side again. I thought I might kiss her, but suddenly felt too shy.

We climbed again, past the quarry cottages and up to the Blue Lagoon. We walked on, in single file again. It was a very warm and lovely day. We went on to Porthgain, then down the steps to the harbour. We reached the pub at lunch time.

We bought sandwiches and halves of cider, wondering, in our conspiracy, if the squares would approve of our drinking halves. We sat at an outside table.

"You've never been on any of the rugby trips, have you?" I asked.

"No. Have you?"

"A couple." I didn't feel a trace of shyness. "There's a song they sing, or we sing, on the bus. 'The sweetest girl I ever saw, Was sipping cider through a straw.'"

We finished the sandwiches and went back for two more halves. Then we talked, briefly, of the squares and then, for quite a while, of what we earnestly referred to as "relationships". I suspect the conversation, whose details have faded in my mind, wouldn't bear much recording and probably would sound a little like the pontificating of a couple of non-drinkers on their second halves of cider. I think we agreed on some ponderous formula about having things in common and then much about sharing things, feeling a kinship.

And then I badly wanted to kiss her, and did so. Her kiss was wary, almost chaste, but it lingered, we lingered, for quite a while.

* * *

It is because of that and other mornings, other days, that I truly believed that, though we were children of the seventies and born into liberated times, we were utterly different, that we had a love which was sacrosanct, aloof from intrigue and affair. And why, when she left me (could there really have been another man? – can you understand that I cannot bring myself to speak or write of this?), that is why, when she left me, I was so lost.

To all intents and purposes, my meaningful life ended when I was thirty-three and Julie left me. And that is why my first and probably only attempt at fiction has been such a lie. My affair, if you can call it that, with Cheryl, has also been a fabrication. For it wasn't, shouldn't be, won't be, an affair. For six weeks now, I have re-invented some of Julie's and my landscapes, imagined Cheryl as Julie. Cheryl is fine, she's friendly, she's nice, but... Come on. I've never kissed her – or held her hand. Or anything. My opening narrative led so easily (and, for me, so sweetly) to the lingering kiss in the lunchtime pub. And that of course was Julie... Julie.

I do not think I shall write any more fiction.

LADIES' MAN

It was nearing ten on a Saturday evening and the cricket club bar was growing noisy with beer. Madeline Hawkins, who had been spending one of her occasional evenings there with her son and daughter, for a bar meal and a couple of bitter lemons, began to feel just a little less than at home.

The door swung open and the bar was exuberantly approached by Gentleman Jim. He'd clearly been home to change since his afternoon's game and, while most of the other players around the bar wore pullovers or casual jackets, Jim was, as often, immaculate in a club blazer, stiff white shirt and, on this occasion, a cravat – at other times it might be one of his many association ties. He seemed to be approaching the barmaid with a view to cashing a fairly large cheque.

His suaveness was so habitual that Madeline was among the few to notice clearly the swagger of Jim's manner at the bar, as he supervised the cashing of his cheque. "Absolutely as it comes to your hand, my dear. Tens, fives, whatever." He was clearly pressing his attentions on a new and pretty young barmaid. A few derisory catcalls came from the players clustered at the bar. The very mildness of the amusement reflected how commonplace such flirtations of Jim's were.

Madeline, though, could only wince, inwardly and sadly. She'd known Jim and his mother for nearly twenty years. It would have been nice simply to enjoy the preposterous and rather caricatured charm of Jim's suaveness but she was only too aware of the rather long and squalid series of affairs which had resulted from Jim's charming approaches. Madeline just didn't like philanderers, and the almost comic quality of Jim's public image and stereotype wasn't enough to make up to Madeline for the painful conviction that, once Jim began his courtships, someone's feelings would eventually get badly hurt.

Madeline next saw Jim about a fortnight later, on a Saturday evening on Paddington Station. She'd spent a couple of days in London at a convention run by the Women's Institute and now, as she was checking the time of the West Wales train, she suddenly noticed Jim, looking considerably scruffier and altogether less suave than usual, standing just outside the buffet. She watched him for a moment, not really wanting to strike up a meeting. He was indeed oddly dishevelled, clad not in one of his frequent blazers, but in a shabby suede windcheater, and without a tie. Madeline was fairly convinced – she'd heard and been told enough of him over the years to feel justified in the conviction – that Jim was now emerging at the end of some protracted debauch. He had regularly been known, or at least had been rumoured, to have had various women in London.

She was at this point in her reflections when Jim noticed her. He seemed to hesitate, then ambled across to her. "Mrs Hawkins, good morning. Are you having a good trip?" Madeline nodded, and Jim pressed on. "I'm desperately sorry to be such a nuisance, but I wonder – well, sadly, I've spent out absolutely, I'm afraid. Could you perhaps lend me forty pence to get a cup of tea?" A little relieved at the innocuousness of the request, Madeline sifted through her purse, while Jim seemed to be struggling to let his now rather bleary charm re-assert itself. "I'm sure this is very inconvenient, Mrs Hawkins. I shall of course repay you promptly once we're back in town." Madeline passed over the forty pence, with little expectation of ever seeing its repayment, and Jim thanked her, before moving slowly off towards the buffet.

A quarter of an hour later, after Madeline was installed on the train, Jim entered her compartment, nodded to her very politely once again, and settled in a corner seat across the way, seemingly to sleep. As the train set off, Madeline puzzled a little about this rather unlikely travelling companion.

He was scruffy that evening, certainly; he clearly hadn't shaved, and his windcheater looked grubby. Jim had married once, and it had lasted only four or five years, although, as Madeline had to admit to herself, the girl had been a flighty piece – Jim may in fact have been more sinned against than sinning. There were rumours as well though, of numerous affairs and liaisons, increasingly later with women rather younger than himself. Admittedly, Madeline was drawing here largely upon stock community gossip, but Jim certainly did have a widespread reputation as a womaniser.

Over the past few years, Madeline had grown to know Jim slightly more at first hand, since her son had been playing cricket for the town club, where Jim was captain of one of the teams. It was the custom to ask players' wives, girl friends and mothers to prepare the teas, on rota, for the home games. Madeline had developed quite an interest in the game, beginning to go along to watch her son even when it wasn't her turn to prepare the teas. And, in this male milieu, Jim was also extravagantly urbane. He had the reputation for being a very good captain and tactician, was apparently quite a reasonable player, and although his projection of the cricketer's image had more of the English public school variety than the homelier local version, he seemed to relate very well and congenially to the other players. Madeline always noticed though, seeming to wink its way, ever present, through the world of the man's man, a deep concern, variously gallant, flirtatious, even on times – and Madeline had to admit this – extremely courteous, a concern for the women who were usually present at the club and its bar. When making arrangements with her for the teas, he was affable and polite; when he came to give her the eight pounds which the club paid the females to cover their expenses, Jim passed it over with an almost ostentatious discretion, in a buff envelope.

He was very gracious towards Madeline, certainly – and, as she reflected, she was ten years older than he. What she didn't like was the more flirtatious aura which would surround Jim when there were other younger women around. With players' wives, he was debonair in a socially acceptable sense. Worse was his attitude to single women. With at least two club barmaids, to Madeline's knowledge, he really had developed a kind of glib charm which always seemed to be moving close to absurdity. She'd found the charm and its implications intensely distasteful.

This view of Jim was very much the widespread one among Madeline's circle, but there was one exception. Madeline's friend Agnes, a woman ten years older than Madeline herself, a widow, a bright and garrulous sixty-five, who prided herself on the broadmindedness of her views. She'd often defended Jim to Madeline in conversation. Agnes had been a close childhood friend of Jim's mother, now dead, and had known him quite well when he was growing up. Jim's father had died very young and he had been brought up in a female household – his mother, an aunt and a housekeeper. He'd also had a spell at a public school. Jim's mother, like her son, had been an extravagant and flamboyant figure. She'd been a feted local soprano and regularly decked herself quite majestically to sing in local arts clubs. She'd been widely known, with a mixture of affection and mockery, as "Songbird".

Agnes always attributed Jim's fascination and fondness for women at least in part to the fact of his having been brought up in an all-female home, and to the powerful and glamorous personality of his mother. She always maintained, very vigorously, that Jim was in fact a "ladies' man" in a much fuller sense than people generally appreciated; that at the heart of his personality there was a deep and genuine affection for the female sex. As for Jim's affairs, well no, Agnes couldn't deny them. She always maintained though that the broken marriage was no fault of Jim's and that, in fact, he never seemed to have got a girl pregnant. Yes, perhaps he was just too careful, but Agnes still insisted that Jim's view of women embraced a real range of emotions: tenderness, regard and affection, as well as the cruder body of male lusts. And that, Madeline would point out, was the problem. "It's a problem, dear, of course," said Agnes, "but that strain is always there, isn't it – with all of them?"

As the evening deepened into night, and the train journeyed West, Jim seemed to rally a little, to look round him rather more brightly. Madeline became a little indignant on noticing that the first signs of real brightening tended to show themselves when women, particularly younger women, passed on and off the train. Jim's seat was facing inwards at the end of the carriage, and Madeline couldn't but notice that, as each new woman walked in and away from him, Jim's eyes would seem to roll tenderly downwards, flickering as his gaze seemed to rest for a second or two on the cast of the girl's buttocks. Madeline was irritated by this rather silly kind of infatuation which men could develop for women younger than themselves.

And then, at Bridgend, the young mother arrived. She was a woman of perhaps twenty-two, twenty-four, struggling with a large suitcase, and two small children, the younger still a baby. She was wretchedly bedraggled: her hair was lank, seemingly uncombed, and she was drably dressed in a black blouse and faded denims. Jim had dashed forward gallantly to lift her suitcase to the rack on her arrival in the compartment, and had helped her stow her pushchair in the corner; thereafter he seemed to peruse her as she smoked one cigarette after another, and struggled to placate her two children, each of whom seemed tired and fractious.

Madeline could only guess at what had brought the girl to these unaccompanied and weary straits. Was she a single parent, maybe? Madeline was used to hearing the phrase "single parent" nowadays, but it was not really of her generation or of her social background. Under different circumstances, or given a slightly less daunting physical appearance on the girl's part, Madeline might have liked to help cheer her up a little, help keep the children amused. But the girl's appearance was ominous, suggestive of Heaven knows what social complications, and Madeline didn't feel it would be appropriate to interfere.

Their train went on to Carmarthen that evening, before they had to disembark and wait for the branch line to Haverfordwest. Jim, who was looking altogether sprucer and fresher now, once again helped the girl with her suitcase and her pushchair, before leaving her installed on a platform bench to wait the half hour before their connection.

Then the drunk appeared: a rather seedy-looking man in a long trench coat. For a while he made sporadic attempts to ingratiate himself with the young mother, clearly to her annoyance – although, to be honest, she looked so world-weary that there was something half-hearted and apathetic in her rejections. Eventually, though, the drunk squatted on a bench beside the mother, and started to play rather inanely with the children, tickling and irritating them. Clearly now, the girl was both distressed and frightened.

At this moment, Jim acted – and Madeline, despite herself, was impressed by the positive social command he suddenly displayed. Briefly, he strode across to the bench.

"Come on now, sunshine. We don't want to have the young lady upset, do we? We mustn't make a nuisance of ourself."

The drunk muttered something about someone lending him a quid for a drink, and Madeline wondered whether Jim would actually buy him off – only to remember that Jim of course had claimed to be quite spent out earlier.

Jim's approach was in fact more imaginative. "Have you tried the Llansteffan Arms? Just across the bridge. They'll usually let you have one on the slate. Yes. Quite honestly. If you leave the entrance there – just over the bridge and up to the left. I should try them."

Madeline assumed this was a fabric of Jim's inventing – she doubted if there was a Llansteffan Arms even. But the ploy seemed to satisfy the drunk who, after a little more argument, hand-shaking and reassurance, seemed ready to set off for the imagined pub. For a while then, he seemed to get sidetracked and confused, and Jim had to prod him on just a shade more firmly. "Come on, sport. Come on now. The young lady really mustn't be bothered. You go and get that drink. That's the lad. Good man." Slowly, the drunk shambled for the station entrance and they saw him no more.

Shortly afterwards, their connection arrived, and Jim helped the girl, with her children, pushchair and suitcase, into a compartment. The girl had said little, even after the encounter with the drunk, save to mumble a rather sheepish word or two of thanks, but she seemed to regard Jim now, perhaps a little hesitantly, as a protector.

The train was a corridor style one, and Madeline followed Jim, the girl and her children into the compartment in which Jim and the girl would otherwise have been alone. Just why she did this, she wasn't too sure herself. Her sense of social propriety had been offended slightly by Jim's aura of protectiveness. She didn't feel it would be altogether suitable for the girl to be alone (children or not) with someone of Jim's reputation. She felt it would be better if there was another woman present – and this despite the fact that her instincts were shrinking a little now from the sense of the socially disreputable which was beginning to surround the whole encounter.

During the forty-minute journey from Carmarthen home, they said little. The girl did tell Jim she had been up in Bridgend for a couple of days to appear in court, but other than that they learned nothing about her. All Madeline could go on really was the abiding impression, from the girl's appearance and the manner of her travelling alone, that she must be socially in difficult, if not actually dubious, circumstances.

Then the girl asked Jim, "What time do we reach Fishguard?"

"Fishguard? There's no connection for Fishguard, I'm afraid. This train gets to Haverfordwest just before midnight."

A confused conversation followed, the girl rather withdrawn and inarticulate. She had to get to Fishguard and the train wasn't going near there. What seemed unsurprising was that she had no money for a taxi. Vaguely, she suggested she might hitch-hike.

Jim's answer to this muddle was a simple and obvious one.

"There's really no problem, my dear. I have my car at the station. I'll drive you up. You really can't be out too much longer now. Those little ones are very tired."

Madeline was frightened and shocked by this suggestion. She really couldn't doubt that Jim would see this intimate late night drive as a possible prelude to... well, what Madeline would call "taking advantage". And even if he didn't... well, it just wasn't proper. It was typical of Jim that he would get mixed up with doubtful sorts of people. And really, Madeline was afraid for the girl. She was sorry for her and seriously alarmed at the thought of her being at the mercy of a man with very few scruples.

For days afterwards, she was to worry over the fact that she did nothing to help the girl herself. Admittedly, she had relatively little money left at the end of the trip, certainly not enough for a taxi, but her husband was meeting her at the station, and they could have driven the girl to Fishguard. Nigel was, of course, a little particular and conservative about giving lifts and certainly wouldn't have appreciated a midnight drive of over thirty miles. That was part of the difficulty. And really, Madeline couldn't blame it all on Nigel. It was just that inner shrinking feeling of her own: the girl looked frankly disreputable, she didn't know what sort of social milieu she'd be getting into. Ultimately, Madeline didn't want to get involved.

None of these notions really eased the alarm which Madeline felt both at the sight and the recollection of Jim ushering the girl and her children quite grandly out of Haverfordwest station and to his car. "You bring the little ones, my dear. Take them along gently, there's no rush. I'll bring the chair and the suitcase, and stow them in the boot."

The whole business stayed uneasily in Madeline's mind for a while, and she told her friend the whole story the next day. Agnes was inclined to take a more charitable view of Jim's involvement in the affair. "I doubt very much, dear, if his intentions would have been at all dubious. Jim's the sort of fellow who really would rally to a damsel in distress."

A week later, Madeline was gazing out of her kitchen window when she saw Agnes bustling excitedly down her drive and brandishing a copy of the local paper. She brought it in.

"This you must see. I think you're going to have to revise one of your opinions. Look at this. Letters to the Editor."

The letter to the local *Argus* was from a clergyman in Cardiff.

I should like to make public my thanks to a good Samaritan – a gentleman, I imagine, from Haverfordwest.

My daughter found herself stranded at Haverfordwest station at midnight last Saturday, with her two small children and no means of getting home to her flat in Fishguard. I am extremely grateful to the gentleman who took care of her during her journey, and drove her and her children to Fishguard. He refused to accept any payment for his petrol, or to leave any name or address so that I might reimburse him myself.

This was a kind and Christian act, something sadly untypical in a world in which so many people are too ready to "pass by on the other side". I hope the gentleman in question reads your paper, will recognise himself, and will accept my sincere thanks for his kindness.

Madeline read this twice, feeling a little sheepish, and a little irritated by Agnes's re-iteration: "Jim really would be kind to a lady in distress, Madeline."

Their reverie was broken by a ring on the doorbell. On the

doorstep, Madeline found Jim: again, as habitually, spruce, blazered and well-groomed.

"Mrs Hawkins. Good morning. I have come to repay a social obligation." He passed her a buff envelope. "You'll remember that you kindly loaned me forty pence for a cup of tea."

And with a smile, with a slight bow almost, Jim had gone. Deftly and crisply, his bright new shoes rattling sharply on the drive, he strode briskly off down the street.

For a long while, Madeline gazed in bewilderment at his retreating figure. She was flooded by a mingling of intense and unexpected emotions: guilt of a kind, gratitude, admiration – and something she recognised, with a sudden shock, as a hidden soft desire.

DORS, MON PETIT, DORS

I was at Victoria in plenty of time when the boat train from Dover got in. Helen appeared, struggling through the crowd with two large suitcases, while the little boy, looking rather travel-weary but quite perky in a way, scurried beside her. Helen looked tired too, but in a deeper, sadder way. She had, after all, years of confusion and frustration behind her. I greeted her, took the suitcases and kissed her quickly on the cheek.

"Hello, Helen. And this must be Pierre."

Helen smiled, "Hello, Uncle Ray. Yes, this is Pierre. He's a little tired now. Are we going straight home?"

I did indeed plan to go straight home. It meant travelling through much of the night, and it would have been easier to stay over in London, but I had a strange, almost superstitious feeling that something might yet go wrong. The arranging that Helen and Pierre should at last come back had been so tortuous and fraught that I was half-fearful still, and hurrying to get on the road West and back to town.

When we got to my car and had stowed the suitcases in the boot, Helen asked, "Could I sit in the back seat with Pierre, Uncle Ray? I must try to get him to sleep."

So we set off for town with the niece I hadn't seen for five years. In the back seat, she nestled the little boy down and, in a low voice, muttered endearments and encouragements, trying to get him off to sleep.

"*Pierre, Pierre. Il faut dormir maintenant. Couche-toi, mon petit, couche-toi.*"

She spoke to me just a little more loudly. "Does the journey take long now, Uncle Ray? There's a lot of motorway now, isn't there?"

"It's not too bad now, Helen. Six hours."

"He can have a good sleep then. *Dors, mon petit, dors.*"

Helen was my brother Ivor's girl. I find it difficult, even now, to talk about the events which led her to France. I find it hard to accept, really, that a cruelty – or was it just a lack of feeling? – that a cruelty such as Ivor's should be so close to me. Even now, it seems scarcely real.

Ivor and I were brought up as strict Nonconformists by a minister father; I suppose there was a liberal sprinkling of the Puritan work ethic and morality in our upbringing. As the younger son, I'd never absorbed it as keenly as Ivor. In any case, the actual Baptist element, the religious quality, was never really oppressive, even with Ivor. His own curious version of the work ethic was a kind of academic one; an Oxford graduate, he became in time the very archetype of the old-style grammar school master. He was strict, censorious and (as slowly and sadly revealed itself over the years, to me and Mandy) obsessed with academic progress and standards.

Ivor's wife died when his two children were very small, and both of them, rather solemn little kids it often seemed, grew up supported by a formidable housekeeper. Mandy and I would take the kids out often, but increasingly, as the years went by, it became difficult to unwind them into the sort of easy rhythm that suits most kids. According to Ivor, they didn't like sweets and they didn't like ice-cream, and Jonathan, the elder one, seemed to be in determined agreement with his father. Sometimes, though, when Helen was still a child, she and I would go for walks along the Frolic and back sometimes to a café in town, where she'd stuff for half an hour at a time on Coke and ice-cream.

As the car drummed onwards down the motorway, with the night now really deep, Helen spoke, unexpectedly.

"How's Aunt Mandy?"

"She's very well. She's been on edge all week waiting for you to arrive."

"She was always very kind. I've missed you both."

There was a pause. We'd missed her – terribly. Mandy and I hadn't been able to have children of our own; this was now approaching the return of our own daughter.

I cast a quick glance at the boy bundled in the corner.

"How's that youngster of yours taking the journey?"

"He's fine. He's sleeping nicely now." She just tucked for a moment at the rug around Pierre. *"Dors, cheri, dors."*

The car raced on.

Jonathan, Ivor's boy had always been his father's son. He was academically brilliant, certainly, and had proceeded to a Cambridge PhD and a university lecturership in tropical medicine. We see very little of him now.

And that left Helen, who wasn't academically brilliant, but she was determined. She did after all go to university. It's just that she needed two attempts at 'A' level to get there, and that her two years studying French at Cardiff were strewn with minor crises. She'd had to re-sit exams both summers and worse (far worse), as far as Mandy and I were concerned, was the suggestion, during her second year, that she might have been mixed up with drugs. It's hard to be certain, because Ivor was censorious and condemning, inclined to hush it up. But it was all beginning to look too much now as if we had the classic story of a youngster rebelling against a parent's pressure.

And so it proved. Helen went off for the year in France which was part of her course, and she never came back. Again, Ivor wasn't sure whether to keep quiet about things or whether to condemn the girl from the rooftops, but in time we learned that she was living with some boyfriend and planning to stay in France. A little while later, we heard about her little boy. And, for Ivor, that was quite emphatically the end of his relationship with his daughter.

And now suddenly, as happens on that road, Port Talbot steelworks were looming, away to our left. And Helen stirred.

"Isn't that a tremendous sight, Uncle Ray?"

I had to agree. "I've always found it moving," I said, "but it's a strange kind of moving, isn't it?"

"Uncle Ray?" She sounded a little anxious. "When I was travelling back to Cardiff... after I'd been down in vacations to see my... father... well, coming back, I found it almost cathartic. You know, it was almost purifying... It's a terrible thing to confess, but I can see things more clearly now, and, well, often I'd gaze at those lights from the train and I'd dream of little secret acts of wickedness. It sounds shameful, doesn't it?"

"It was quite understandable."

"I suppose so. For years I'd been reacting against my... father." That was the second time she'd hesitated before using the word "father". The cathartic pull of the steelworks seemed to be drawing confession from her.

"Did he tell you I was on drugs for a while?"

"Yes."

"I'm sorry. I said that partly to shock, I think. In a silly way. To be honest, it was a very mild flirtation with cannabis. Just a sort of anti-my father thing. I didn't really rebel, not just then. Not till I got to France."

"And how was France, Helen?"

"A relief, really. I felt really bitter when I went out. So I found a boyfriend fairly soon, which was incredibly silly, looking back. He was little better than a gigolo and he'd left me within six months. Then it was just me and Pierre, but even that was free, and a relief of a kind. But I started to get this pull, towards home... only home was you and Aunt Mandy, of course. And then, when you wrote and said my... father had left, I started really wanting to come home." She paused a little lamely. "So here we are." Pierre, perhaps disturbed a little by the flurry of talking, stirred in his sleep. *"Dors, Pierre. Dors, cheri, dors."*

Ivor had left town a year earlier. Obviously, being a grammar school teacher had always been a little below his personal aspirations and when Ivor saw the era of the comprehensive school looming in the near future he set out to find his own way to the academic pinnacle. He'd worked on his MEd and his PhD and had reached the summit a year before: a senior lectureship in educational studies at Oxford. With Jonathon in London and Helen gone, Ivor sold up and left Haverfordwest, seemingly for ever.

It took Mandy and me a year's letter-writing to persuade Helen that the coast was clear. And here we were, driving off the motorway and on to the roads of Carmarthenshire. From the back seat came the soft sound of Pierre's deep breathing and his mother's whispered lullaby.

The next eighteen months, nearly two years, were an extraordinary, almost idyllic, interlude. To strike a selfish note:

Mandy and I were host to a niece whom we had come to think of as a daughter, and a three year-old who rapidly seemed to regard himself as a grandson. It was Helen herself, in fact, who at once encouraged him to call us "Granny" and "Grandad." She and Mandy used to sit with the boy for hours early on, naming things for him, because for much of the time in France, she'd talked to him in French. She'd felt it would be less complicated that way. In French, she said, she could feel more easily freed from the world of her father. In French they were secret and safe. But she had still wanted to come home.

I have so many clutching memories of those two years. Mandy had given up her job as an infant teacher, and Helen in time found a clerical job in the local planning office, so that Mandy was together a great deal with her new grandson. Often, at weekends and in the evenings, I would take Pierre for walks over to the Picton playing field for embryonic games of football and cricket. I would go out to meet Pierre and Helen as they walked back from the corner grocery shop late some afternoons. Sometimes I'd take Pierre with me into town on the bus. For the first time, I experienced that strange foreshortening of perspective that comes from viewing the world again through the eyes of a small child. Once Pierre was standing to look out of the front window of our doubledecker and, pointing out, he exclaimed. "This is our town, isn't it, Grandad?"

Then we heard that Ivor was coming back. Expanding into his role as a cosmopolitan academic he was planning to buy a holiday cottage just outside Haverfordwest and would be down with us fairly regularly in vacations. Maybe he hoped also to resume his contact with Helen; it's hard to say because his letter just said something incredibly pompous about "this being the time for forgiveness." It is just possible, though, that he was hankering a little more than he'd expected for his native patch, and that Helen's presence there was largely incidental. It's hard to say. Either way, Ivor would soon be with us again. We waited, in a mood of sick tension, for his arrival.

Mandy and I got in, around four one evening, to find that Helen and Pierre had packed and gone. She'd left just a short note:

My dear Ray and Mandy,
I'm sure you'll understand. I just can't face seeing him again. If I could, I would, and I don't want to go, but it seems the only way. Pierre and I will go to London. When things have settled down, I will write. Please don't feel I'm walking out on you. I love you both. I and Pierre love you both. But please don't try to follow us. I will write in time.

All my love,
Helen.

In the turmoil of the next hour, I thought of the station and set off there, in search of them. As I got on to the platform, the train was waiting to leave, and Helen and Pierre were in a corner seat. After I'd sat opposite Helen and Pierre in their compartment, we said little. The train was ready to pull out and I'd have to travel with them at least part of the way. Both Helen and I seemed to realise this, and the train had in fact left the station before either of us spoke. Nervously, Helen lit the first cigarette I'd seen her smoke since she'd come home. At last, I started the conversation.

"Please stay. Please change your mind."

She stubbed out the cigarette. "Ray, I can't. I thought you might guess and come to the train, but… please try to accept it."

I tried again. "I'm sure your father is genuine in wanting to see you again. And it wouldn't be too regular, Helen. Just now and again. Isn't it better sometimes… forgive and forget? Or… that's a little clumsy, but…"

She looked down sadly, and then Pierre, who'd looked wide-eyed and confused throughout, spoke for the first time. "Is Grandad coming with us, Mummy?"

It would have been possible, I suppose, to bring the argument back to Pierre: should he lose a new home for the sake of the occasional unpleasantness? But I couldn't feel that was a fair way to argue. So I just said, "I'm coming as far as Swansea with you, Pierre. And then we'll see."

We said little or nothing for a long while. Then Helen said, "Ray. There's just one thing… you said 'forgive and forget'." She was fidgeting with a loose buckle on her raincoat. "Just before I went to France, when I'd had a re-sit and it wasn't long after the drugs business… well, I was really in disgrace. I mean, he'd always made me think I wasn't worthy to be his daughter – there was that sort of mood about it all. And he'd always say I was just like my mother." She paused and fumbled for a cigarette packet again, only she didn't smoke another, just kept twisting and turning the packet in her hands. "It made me really long for my mother sometimes. But then – it was just before I went to France – he said I was my mother's daughter: he often said that. And he started abusing her, as a slut and things like that, and he said I wasn't his daughter. Jonathan was his son, he said, but I wasn't his daughter. And… it was a weird conversation, as if fact and metaphor were getting mixed… but he did call me a bastard, and that was the first time he'd ever said that. He didn't often swear. But that's what he felt, clearly." Fiercely she crumpled the cigarette packet and hurled it to the corner of the compartment. "Ray… you can't say forgive and forget. There are some things, really there are, which shouldn't be forgiven."

Pierre started to cry. Helen slid an arm around him and nuzzled him gently. Slowly, with my mind lurching around the pointless details of train times, I just said, "There's about ten minutes, after we get to Swansea, before the Inter-City leaves. I'll see you on to it, and get you all tucked up. It'll be a long journey for Pierre."

At Swansea that night, the wide and open doors of the waiting Inter-City just looked frightening and swallowing. I saw Helen and Pierre to their compartment, and tried to stumble over the usual platitudes.

"You know that we'll always love you."

"Of course. I will write. And I'll try to come and see you again. Honestly. It isn't quite goodbye."

And then Pierre, who was wrapped in a light rug in the corner, whimpered softly. Then he just said, "*Maman*" – he seemed unable to say any more. It was as if he was caught now between two languages and there were literally no words in which he could express himself and his misery. Very carefully and gently, Helen stroked back his hair. "*Couche-toi, Pierre. Il faut dormir maintenant. Dors, cheri, dors.*"

And I was aware then that the conversation was over. I kissed Helen gently on the cheek, and leaned over to kiss Pierre too, very softly, so as not to disturb him. "Goodbye, Helen," I said. "I know you will write."

"Of course I will," she said. Then Pierre stirred again and Helen turned back to him. "*Couche-toi, cheri. Dors, mon petit, dors.*"

I left the compartment, slow and confused, and made for my platform and the next train home.